Hat City
Publishing

# TRACKING ARIANA

A Dan Burnett Thriller

## BY

# LARRY TERHAAR

# CHAPTER 1

At 4:00 p.m. on April 27, 2025, Ariana Wilkinson was exiting Pascone Park in Ardsley, New York. She and her children, three-year-old Katie, and Joseph Jr., who was one and a half, had attended an Eid celebration sponsored by The Muslim Center, a mosque in Mt Vernon. She'd been a member of the congregation for three years, ever since coming to America from Afghanistan. This was the mosque's annual family outing, and her kids had enjoyed a myriad of outdoor games. They'd jumped into a pool of plastic balls, bounced in an inflatable castle, and had their faces painted. The day had been perfect: bright, sunny, and warm for that time of year.

Ariana was pushing Joey in a stroller, while Katie walked alongside proudly displaying a flower painted high on her right cheek. They paused along the path to watch two boys fishing in a brook.

"Look, Mommy, he caught one," Katie exclaimed, pointing to one of the boys as his rod bent and began wiggling as he reeled in a small fish.

Kneeling down to meet Katie's face, Ariana said, "See the orange on the fish's belly? I think that's a Sunny."

Katie was fascinated as they watched for a few more moments while the boys removed the hook and let the fish splash back into the water, maybe to be caught again.

Pushing a stroller had become Ariana's main source of exercise since becoming a mom. She was a small woman, barely over five feet, but she was strong. With dark eyes, elegant features, and an exotic complexion, she was striking to those who passed by. As they turned the corner onto the sidewalk, Ariana froze. Less than a block ahead, she saw two men dressed in official-looking black attire. *Dammit. I let my guard down, and here I am wearing a hijab, something I never do in public,* she scolded herself.

Ever since she was thirteen, going to school in Afghanistan, she always looked ahead before turning a corner, with an eye out for danger. After three years in the States, she was about to pay the price for becoming soft. If she were not with her children, Ariana would have run. Run like she and her friends had run so many times from the Taliban. As the men approached, she saw the ICE identification on their jackets. Ariana's heart raced, and her nose flared with her quickening breath.

"Excuse me, Ma'am, can you show us some identification?" In addition to his words, the body language that exuded from these men was intimidating. Attempting to calm her nerves, she took a deep breath and recalled how she and the other Muslim mothers had prepared for a confrontation like this ever since the election. Ariana reached into her purse, removed her Green Card, New York driver's license, and her children's U.S. birth certificates. After handing them to the man who spoke to her, she stood silently, confident that she had presented proper identification.

After each of the men viewed their IDs, carefully comparing the driver's license photo with her face, the same man asked, "Where are you from, ma'am?"

"New Rochelle," Ariana replied respectfully.

"No. I mean, where were you born?"

"Afghanistan. My husband brought me here three years ago, after the war."

"Was he in the military?"

"Yes, sir. He still is. I can assure you I am here legally."

"You're going to need to come with us so we can confirm all that."

It was then that she noticed other members of her mosque going through the same questioning alongside a van with Immigration and Customs Enforcement stenciled on the side. With her heart still pounding, she focused on her breathing, trying to prevent a full-blown panic attack. "Where are you taking us?" Ariana rasped.

"Just to the local police station for an interview."

"Is there a problem with our identification, Sir?"

"That's not for me to decide. I'm sure we'll get this cleared up, and you can be on your way."

Without another word, Ariana and her children followed one man to the van while the other trailed closely behind. There, she folded Joey's stroller and climbed into the packed van as others made room for them.

"Why are we in this truck, Mommy?" Katie asked.

"I don't know, sweetie. They said we need to be interviewed."

"What does interviewed mean?"

"Questions. They want to ask us some questions. Don't worry, I'm sure we'll be home in time for dinner."

Katie looked up at her mom, trying to make sense of what she said. As the doors slammed shut, every adult inside the van silently glanced at each other, fearing the worst. Ariana held her children close, trying to imagine what was in store for them.

SETH BODNER ARRIVED at his law office at 8:00 a.m. on Monday, his usual arrival time. He liked to have an hour of peace to organize his thoughts and prepare for the day before the phone started ringing and his appointments began. Once he'd started a pot of coffee in the break room, he moved to his desk to listen to voicemails. The third message caught his attention: "Mr. Bodner, this is Imam Khan at the Westchester Muslim Center. Some members of our congregation were detained by ICE agents on Sunday while leaving our annual Eid festival. Please return my call at your earliest convenience."

Providing pro bono legal services to local religious organizations was something Seth had been doing ever since he began his practice. Typically, these services included guidance on nonprofit organizations, real estate transactions, and ensuring tax compliance. This was the first time he'd been asked about immigration enforcement.

While pouring himself a cup of coffee, Seth recalled his brief time as a public defender—his first job after passing the bar exam. He fondly remembered the sense of accomplishment he'd felt helping people down on their luck—people who'd been trapped in a legal system with no money and nowhere else to turn. Once he'd hung up a shingle, he found himself chasing money, or at least working for people who had some.

Looking forward to helping those in need, he returned the call. "Yes, Imam, Seth Bodner here. How are you today?"

"I'm fine. It's my congregation that I'm concerned about," he said wearily.

"Tell me what happened."

"Yesterday, at Pascone Park, a number of our congregants were taken into custody after our annual family celebration. No one has heard from them, and we don't know where they are."

"Is there anything else you can tell me?"

"Some other festival goers saw them leave in an Immigration and Customs Enforcement van. We need to locate them."

"All right, I'll make some calls and see what I can find out. I'll get back to you soon."

"Thanks, Mr. Bodner."

As Seth sat back in his chair, wondering where to start, his legal assistant entered the office, hung up her jacket, and headed for the coffee pot. "Good morning, Seth. How was your weekend?"

"Fine, Paula. But it seems some congregants of the Westchester Muslim Center were picked up by ICE yesterday in Ardsley. So far, no one knows where they are."

Cocking her head, Paula tried to comprehend what she'd just heard, then asked, "Have the local police been informed?"

"I was just about to contact them."

"I'll make the call for you."

A few moments later, Paula announced, "I have Lieutenant Davies of the Ardsley police on line one."

"Thanks, I'll want to speak with Congressman Latimer next."

"Got it."

After clearing his throat, Seth pressed line one and said, "Good morning, Lieutenant. What do you know about some members of the Muslim center being picked up by ICE yesterday?"

"Let me first say that this department played no role in the detentions. Twelve people were picked up by ICE and held here overnight. They've since been transported to the Orange County Correction Center."

"Can you provide me with a list of names?"

"Well, this was an ICE operation all the way. We were merely cooperating by letting them use our facilities."

"I understand, Lieutenant. But I still need a list of names."

"I'll see what I can do. Give me your fax number."

After reciting both the phone and fax numbers, Seth said, "Thank you, Lieutenant. I'll be standing by." He then buzzed Paula, "Any luck with Congressman Latimer?"

"I have his secretary on line two."

"Good morning. Attorney Bodner for the congressman," Seth stated flatly, already tired of the telephone protocol.

"Yes, just a moment, please."

"Hello, Seth. What can I do for you on this fine day?"

"Good morning, George. Are you aware that ICE picked up a dozen Muslims yesterday in Ardsley and is detaining them at Orange County Correctional?"

"This is the first I've heard of it. Do you know why?"

"Nobody seems to know anything. I'm waiting for a list of names from Lieutenant Davies with the Ardsley Police."

"Okay, I'll put a call into Orange County. Let's stay in touch on this."

"Good, George. We'll talk soon."

As Seth pondered his next move, Paula walked into his office and handed him the fax from Ardsley P.D. It was a few pages, with twelve names, ages, and home addresses. While perusing the fax, he was startled to see children listed, one just a year old. He immediately called Imam Khan.

# CHAPTER 2

As Colonel Joseph Wilkinson exited the rear of the C-17 military transport aircraft, he set his duffel on the tarmac and stretched his arms overhead. Nine hours in what qualified as a seat had taken its toll on his body. After a few deep knee bends, he picked up his bag and headed inside the hangar, looking forward to seeing his wife and children. He had dreamed of this moment ever since learning his official date of discharge from the Air Force. After eight deployments and twenty years of service, he was about to retire with a full pension.

At just forty-two years old, tall, fit, and in perfect health, he still had most of his life ahead of him—time for a second career, and time to raise a family. While he had gotten to know his daughter, Katie, pretty well, he'd only seen his son for a few days, nearly a year ago.

Inside the hangar at Stewart Field, wives and families welcomed their returning soldiers in a joyous reunion as Joe's eyes searched the crowd for Ariana, Katie, and Joe Jr. He made his way through the sea of people, but still unable to find them, he assumed they'd been stuck in traffic. Joe stepped outside, hoping to catch a glimpse of their arrival.

He tried calling Ariana's cell, but after a few rings, it went to voicemail. Twenty minutes later, as the party was winding down, Captain Slater approached Joe arm in arm with his fiancée and asked, "Do you need a ride, Colonel?"

"I might, Rob. I was expecting my wife and kids, but there's no sign of them."

"Probably just New York traffic. We'll be happy to give you a lift."

"That's nice of you. I'm sure you two had other plans for your reunion." He smiled.

"Hey, we've been waiting a year. What's another hour?" Rob laughed. "This is Allison, by the way."

"I'm happy to meet you, Allison. Rob speaks highly of you."

"Likewise, Colonel. I'm parked right over here," she said, pointing to a Toyota SUV.

Forty-five minutes later, they arrived at Joe's rental house in New Rochelle. As he thanked them for the ride, Rob exclaimed, "Happy retirement, Colonel!"

Joe lugged his bag to the front door, dug out a key buried deep in his wallet, and went inside. With no signs of life, he wandered to the garage and found it empty. Now, certain they were caught in traffic, he tried calling Ariana again. When it went to voicemail, he left a message that he was home and couldn't wait to see them.

He wandered through the house, admiring the comfortable home that Ariana had made for them in his absence. He'd only been here briefly when they moved in a year ago after Joe Jr. was born. He plopped his bag on the bed, then went into the kids' rooms, hoping to get a feel of their lives. Katie's room had lavender walls covered with posters of cartoon characters, her bed piled high with stuffed animals. Joe smiled to himself when he realized the room somehow smelled like a little girl. Or maybe it was bubble gum.

He entered Jr.'s room, painted blue with Sesame Street characters on the walls, and a New York Yankees poster over the crib. There was a changing table along one wall, where he caught the scent of baby wipes. While that was preferable to the other possibility, Joe felt remiss for not being there for the first year of Joey's life.

Still in uniform, Joe made his way to the kitchen, popped open a beer, and stepped out onto the back deck. After his first sip, he was struck by how flavorless the beer was. Over the last year, he'd become accustomed to the rich taste of German brews at the Air Base in Rammstein. He wandered out into the fenced yard, where the grass was soft and moist from April rain. He smiled when he saw fresh buds on the trees, and imagined having cookouts in the yard and playing with his kids. He'd often envisioned playing catch with his son, and wondered how old he'd need to be to throw a baseball.

As Joe approached the fence, he noticed a woman working in the garden next door and called out to her, "Hello there. You must be my neighbor."

The woman stood, removed her gloves, stroked a few strands of hair from her face, and exclaimed, "You're home! Ariana told me you were coming home this week." As she approached the fence, she said, "I'm Liz, by the way," and reached out to shake hands.

"Pleased to meet you, Liz. Have you seen my family today?" Joe asked. "They were supposed to meet me at the air base."

Liz's face sank with concern as she gathered her thoughts. "Oh my. Could they have been at the Eid festival in Ardsley yesterday?"

"I have no Idea. I was in Germany yesterday."

"I hate to tell you this, but there was an ICE raid at the festival. It's been on the news all day. The reports are that they picked up a dozen immigrants, some of them were children."

Frowning, Joe said, "Ariana wouldn't have been picked up—she's here legally. Our children were born here—they're not immigrants."

"Yes, I know. Maybe you should check the news coverage or call some friends," she said cautiously, loath to be the one to inform him.

"Thank you, Liz. I'll do that right now."

As Joe turned toward the house, he thought, *I don't know any friends here.*


**ONCE INSIDE, JOE** turned on the TV and scrolled through the channels looking for anything that appeared to be news. Too anxious to sit, he paced the room, waiting for the commercials to end while running his fingers through his close-cropped hair. Becoming impatient, he continued scrolling through the channels until he caught a glimpse of a woman wearing a hijab. He turned up the volume and listened as she described the raid, "They were waiting outside the festival for us to leave, and were checking IDs. Then they loaded people into a van until it was full and drove away."

The coverage then went to Imam Khan of the Westchester Muslim Center. Listening intently, Joe was surprised to see the man in street clothes, having always pictured Imams wearing robes and prayer caps. While he'd never met the Imam, he knew that Ariana was a member of his congregation. Joe and Ariana had lengthy telephone discussions over the recent years about how much to involve the children in the Muslim faith. It was their mutual decision not to push any religion on them, but to let them be exposed to it as they became older. At their young age, it was not yet an issue.

Joe continued watching as the Imam spoke until he announced that he had a list of people who'd been detained and would share the names with any concerned family members if they called the Mosque. Joe immediately called the number, only to get a busy signal. After a few deep breaths to calm himself, he tried the number again. Still busy. Unwilling to just wait, Joe decided to go to the mosque and speak to the Imam in person. Not having a car, he called an Uber.

After pacing in the driveway for ten minutes, the driver arrived, and they were off to Mt. Vernon. With Joe still in uniform, the driver asked about the ribbons and medals on his chest. While being respectful, he made it clear that he'd rather not talk about them and remained silent, deep in thought, the rest of the way.

Joe wondered how it was possible that his family was detained, despite doing everything the right way, by the book. For over a century, American military men have married foreign women. There were procedures for repatriating them to the United States, and he and Ariana had followed them to the letter.

His mind wandered back to his first introduction to the Muslim faith when he arrived in Afghanistan with the 455th Air Wing. He'd met many people of various religions during other deployments, but that was his first experience working with Muslims. He found them to be calm, practical, almost introverted people who welcomed them into their country with open arms.

It was there that he met Ariana. As one of the higher-ranking officers at Bagram Airbase, he often required an interpreter and assistance with local intelligence. Ariana had been assigned to him, and over time, he learned that as a teenager, she had defied the local authorities and attended Kabul University, something her mother would never have dreamed of. When she'd finished there, she enrolled in the American University, where she was recruited as a military aide. After working together for nearly a year, a romance blossomed between them. Before long, they fell in love and were married. When the American involvement in the war was nearing the end, they began planning how to get Ariana out of Afghanistan, where they knew the Taliban would torture her or even kill her for assisting the Americans. By the time Ariana's evacuation plans were in place, she was expecting a child, and they were both thrilled that the birth would take place in the United States.

That was more than three years ago. After the war ended, Joe was stationed in the States for a year, where he lived near the airbase with Ariana and witnessed Katie's birth. Over the last two years, he'd been flying missions in various places throughout the world, then coming home to Ariana in between tours of duty. It was during one of those homecomings that Joe Jr. was conceived. His last tour was in Germany, at the European Headquarters in Rammstein, where he achieved the rank of full bird Colonel before completing his twenty years of service.

**THE UBER DRIVER** dropped him off at the Muslim Center, where Joe paused with his phone, leaving a five-star rating and a tip, before walking up the steps and entering the building. Beyond the foyer was a large space for prayer, without the church pews common to Christian places of worship. Although a prayer session was not currently taking place, Joe saw a few people kneeling on mats. On each side of the foyer was a hallway, one side leading to classrooms and the other led to offices. As he headed toward the offices with hat in hand, a woman stopped Joe and offered directions.

"Yes. I'm looking for Imam Khan. I'm hoping he knows the whereabouts of my family."

"Were they at the festival yesterday?"

"That's what I'm trying to determine. I tried calling, but the line was busy."

"Follow me, sir."

"Thank you," Joe replied. They made their way down the hall to a waiting area outside an ornate door, likely ancient.

"Who shall I say is calling?" the woman asked.

"Joe Wilkinson. My wife, Ariana, is a member here."

"He'll be with you in a moment, Sir."

Joe waited patiently in a chair, a skill he'd learned repeatedly in the military—a life of hurry up and wait. He scrolled through his phone, still hoping for a message from Ariana. A few minutes later, he was greeted by the Imam. "Mr. Wilkinson?"

"Yes, Sir," Joe replied while standing and offering his hand. "Thank you for seeing me."

"Thank you for your service to our country. Is it Colonel?" Imam Khan asked while shaking hands.

"Very good. Could you tell by the eagle insignia?"

"Actually, Ariana told me you're a Colonel." He chuckled. "She shared her excitement about your homecoming with everyone. Please come in and have a seat."

Joe followed Imam Khan into his office and sat facing his desk. Mounted on the wall behind him was a large Arabesque design. Glancing around the rather plain, white room, he noticed a lectern with a large, gold-trimmed copy of the Quran lying open, alongside a floor-mounted compass. Having spent much of his life with a compass, Joe noted that this one was pointing east, toward Mecca, not to the north.

"So, I'm sure you're here about your family. I'm sorry to inform you that their names are on the list of detainees I received this morning. It's my understanding that they're being held at the Orange County Correction Center."

"Why have they been detained?"

"That we don't know. Since it was a homeland security operation, I can only assume they were targeting Muslims."

"But my children are US citizens, and Ariana is here legally. She has a Green Card."

"Yes, I'm aware of that. We have an attorney looking into the matter as we speak. Perhaps you'd like to talk with him yourself?"

"Definitely."

Imam Khan lifted a business card off his desk and handed it to Joe. "I don't know how much progress he's made already, but I'm sure you'll find him helpful."

"Thank you, I'll call him right away. Before I go, might you know where Ariana's car is parked? It's not in our garage."

"Most of our congregants drove themselves to the festival. It's probably near the park entrance. I can have someone drive you there to look."

"Oh, that would be great. We just have the one car."

The Imam picked up the phone and used the intercom to arrange the ride. A moment later, there was a light knock on the door, and a young man entered. The Imam said, "James, will you give Colonel Wilkinson a ride up to Pascone Park to retrieve his wife's car?"

"I'd be happy to."

After shaking hands with Imam Khan, Joe followed James outside to his car, and they rode together to the park. Just a block from the entrance, Joe spotted Ariana's Honda Accord parallel-parked along the road. "There it is," he said, pointing. "Just give me a minute to see if there's still a spare key."

Joe exited James' car, knelt down at the rear of the Honda, and located a magnetic key holder under the bumper. Holding it up for James to see, he waved as the young man drove away. When Joe sat down in the driver's seat, he smiled at the two child seats strapped in the back—one faced forward, the other facing to the rear. He then fished the attorney's card from his pocket and punched in the number.

"Attorney Bodner's office," a woman's voice answered.

After Joe identified himself and stated the reason for his call, the voice on the line said, "Mr. Bodner is at the Correction Center now. I'm Paula. I'll reach him on his cell and have him call you back. I'm sure he'd like to speak with you."

"Thanks, I'll be at this number."

"Okay, Colonel. You'll hear from him soon."

When the call ended, Joe sat there, not knowing what to do. He thought about driving home, but that might put him further away from where he might need to go next. Perhaps he'd meet with the attorney, or maybe he'd drive up to Orange County himself, to see his family. Having never been to a civilian prison before, he had no idea if he could visit them unannounced. As his anxiety continued to build, he performed breathing exercises to calm himself as he attempted to think positively.

But the longer he waited for the callback, the anxiety resurfaced as he imagined what his family was going through. When he realized twenty minutes had gone by, Joe decided to drive to the prison, hoping for the best—he was desperate to see his loved ones.

With the prison's address entered into a phone app, he pulled away from the curb and headed for Orange County. The app indicated the drive would be an hour, mostly north after crossing the Hudson River. His anxiety subsided slightly as he was at least doing something, *not just waiting around!*

While crossing the Mario Cuomo Bridge, his phone buzzed. "Hello?"

"Colonel Wilkinson? Seth Bodner calling."

"Yes, Mr. Bodner. Thanks for the call."

"I've seen and spoken with your family, and can assure you they're fine."

Relieved, Joe sighed, "What's going on?"

"It seems Washington has a burr up its ass this week for Muslims. There was another raid in Virginia this morning."

"You're aware my wife is here legally, and our children are US citizens?"

"I am. Fortunately, Ariana carries all the documentation with her."

"Good, we've planned for events like this ever since the election."

"Look, I can have the children released to you anytime. The only reason they're being held is that they were with Ariana and had no one else to care for them. Where are you?"

"On my way to Orange County, ETA 3:15."

"Great. I'll start the release process now. Park in the visitors' lot and call me at this number when you arrive. I'll try to arrange for you to see your wife while you're here."

"Thanks. I'll see you in forty-five minutes."

ARIANA HAD COOPERATED with the ICE officers in every way. When they arrived at the Ardsley Police station, she was interviewed again, feeling sure that they would be released after reviewing her documents for the second time. After the interview was over, she and her children were led to a cell of their own, crushing her hopes. Later, she watched as a few of the other detainees were released from adjacent cells, certain she would be next.

Her focus was on keeping her children's spirits up. Fortunately, she'd been allowed to keep the diaper bag, which, besides diapers and formula bottles, contained some snacks for her and Katie. Ariana taught Katie some songs to sing, which fascinated Joey and helped pass the time. Eventually, the children fell asleep, and Ariana began to lose hope of being released that night. With no windows or any other way to tell time, she relied on her body clock to keep track of the passing hours. She bided her time by saying prayers on her knees with nothing but a spare diaper between her legs and the cold concrete.

Her mind drifted back to Afghanistan, where she recalled telling her parents that she'd be leaving for America. While they were initially upset, it wasn't long before they became happy for her. Ariana was the first in their family to get an education, and now that she had an American husband and a baby on the way, they knew it was for the best. They loved Joe, and having a grandchild born in America was a dream come true. Yet they still cried when it became time for her to leave.

Ariana's flight to the United States was on a chartered airline with other family members of American military personnel. Every last seat was filled, and the flight to New York lasted eighteen hours with a stop in Germany for fuel and a crew change. Thankful to have a window seat where she could rest her head, Ariana knew her life was about to change dramatically, her dreams of motherhood fueling her contentment.

**ARIANA MUST HAVE** fallen asleep in the cell at some point during the night because she was startled when the lights came on, and people began moving around. Ariana hoped her captors had come to their senses and decided to release them. But when she, her children, and everyone else were led outside in the dark to a waiting prison bus, her heart sank once again.

# CHAPTER 3

Joe called Attorney Bodner as soon as he arrived at the Correctional Facility—a massive concrete structure in a big field, set well back from the road. It was surrounded by a tall chain-link fence with coils of razor wire on top.

"Hi, Colonel. I believe I have everything set for you. Can you see the visitors' entrance from where you're parked?"

"I can."

"I'll be waiting for you just inside the door."

Joe climbed out of the car, locked the doors, and headed for the entrance. Inside, a blond man in a blue suit approached him as he entered. The man looked too young to be an attorney.

"Colonel Wilkinson?" the man asked, extending his hand.

"Yes, Mr. Bodner, I assume?"

"That's right. I know you were expecting someone older."

"You got me there." Joe smiled. "Please call me Joe."

"And I'm Seth. Follow me."

Both men had to empty their pockets before going through a magnetometer. Once cleared to enter, Joe followed Seth to a visitation area. Because this was a minimum security area, they walked into a sitting room where Ariana and the kids were waiting. With Joe

Jr. in her arms, Ariana rushed toward her husband and wrapped her arms around him, pinning Jr. between them. Katie followed close behind, hugging her father's legs. After kissing his wife, Joe took the boy from her arms and bent down to greet Katie, overjoyed to see them. As Joe embraced his children, Ariana burst into tears, having not seen her husband in a year.

While Joe comforted his wife, Seth said, "I'll leave you to get reacquainted. You have ten minutes until they come for Ariana."

The four of them sat on a vinyl couch, and while Katie clung to her father, Jr. climbed back into his mother's arms, unfamiliar with the strange man before him.

Joe tenderly brushed Ariana's hair from her face and looked into her eyes.

"Are you okay?" he asked.

"I'm scared, Joe. Why are they keeping me here?"

"I can't answer that, honey. Did you get any sleep last night?"

"A little. We had our own cell with two beds, but there was a lot of commotion all night."

"Did Seth explain that I'd be taking the kids home with me?"

"Yes. I wrote out a list of things you'll need to know."

With his arm around her, Joe pulled Ariana close and held her as she wept. The four of them clung to one another and remained that way until Seth returned.

"Listen, they'll be in to take Ariana back in a few minutes. I've been working all day to arrange a formal hearing in front of an Immigration judge, and I've managed to get one scheduled for tomorrow morning. Up until now, I've been representing everyone who was picked up at the park. A few people have asked me to contact their own attorneys, which I've done. Do you have anyone you'd prefer to have represent you?"

Joe looked at Ariana as she shook her head. "No. We've never needed an attorney."

"Okay, I'll represent you. You'll be pleased to know that there will be no charge. Places of worship are my one pro bono cause."

Just then, two guards entered the room, one male and one female, to take Ariana away. Katie began to cry, and Joe Jr. desperately clung to his mother, unwilling to let go. Joe pulled him away as gently as he could, but Jr. began kicking and screaming as his father tried to comfort him. Joe wondered how long it would take for his son to accept him. Unable to do anything else, the family watched as the guards led Ariana away.

Once she was gone, Katie picked up the diaper bag her mother had left behind. As Seth led them outside, he said, "I'll call you tonight when I know the schedule for tomorrow, and don't hesitate to call if there's anything I can help with."

"Thanks for everything, Seth."

"Good luck, Colonel."

Jr. was inconsolable on the way to the car. Once there, Joe stood outside the door, continuing his attempt to comfort him. While holding the boy to his chest, he bounced up and down, humming a lullaby until Jr. began to calm. But when Joe had them both strapped into their car seats, Jr. began to fuss again, and Katie said, "He might need a bottle, Daddy."

Joe looked in the bag and found a bottle of formula ready to go. Leaning inside the car door, he placed the bottle to Jr.'s mouth and was happy to see him reach for it, holding it to his lips. The boy became instantly silent as he greedily nursed the bottle.

Smiling, Joe said, "Thanks, Katie. I'm going to need your help to get through this."

"Don't worry, Daddy. I help mommy with Joey all the time."

"That's good news, honey. Thank you."

IT WAS AN hour's drive to their home, and Joe carried on a conversation with Katie the whole way while Jr. slept. Gazing at her in the rearview mirror, he was enamored with her little face and how her dark brown pig-tails bounced when they went over a bump. He recalled how, when Katie was Jr.'s age, he and Ariana would often take her for a car ride to help her fall asleep.

When they reached the house, Joey woke up when the car stopped moving. Once inside, Joe placed him in a playpen with some toys, while Katie turned on the TV and watched cartoons. With both children occupied, Joe sat down at the kitchen table and read Ariana's note:

*Dear Joe,*

*This is not how I imagined your homecoming. I pictured hours in bed, making love and holding each other. Sorry about that. I know you'll be overloaded with caring for the children, so the next few pages are lists of things you'll need to know. Katie will be a good helper! Hopefully, I'll be released tomorrow, and you'll only have to carry the load for one day.*

*I love you,*

*Ariana*

There were three more pages of notes, schedules, and where to find things. After going through the lists, Joe felt more confident that he could handle it. At least for a day.

LATER THAT EVENING, Seth called, "How are you making out, Joe?"

"Not too bad. We've all eaten, and Jr. is asleep. Ariana left me detailed instructions."

"Good to hear. Regarding tomorrow, the hearing is scheduled for 10:00. It would be best if you wear your uniform and bring the children. Is that doable?"

"Sure, we can handle that."

"Good. With any luck, you'll be taking Ariana home with you. I can't imagine that any Judge in the State of New York will hold a lawful permanent resident in custody, especially one with a decorated military spouse and children who are United States citizens."

"That's good to hear, Seth. I'll call you when we're there."

"Okay, Joe. Sleep well."

With that, Joe tucked Katie into bed and read her a story, something he had dreamed of doing for a year. Once she'd fallen asleep, he tiptoed out of her room, unpacked and laid out his clothes for the next day, and collapsed into bed. Comforted by the scent of his wife on the sheets, his mind drifted back to the first time he experienced that scent.

AFTER A PARTICULARLY stressful day for both of them at the Bagram Airbase, Joe invited Ariana to join him at the officers' club. There, over a beer for him and a Coke for her, they enjoyed a light supper and rehashed the day's challenges. She also opened up a bit about her life, her family, and how she managed to attend school, a rarity for a woman in Afghanistan. Joe found himself enchanted by her smile and captivated by her story. After eating, while walking back to her dorm, she held his hand, the first physical contact between them. Once there, she hugged him goodnight, and it was then that he caught her scent for the first time—faint and mysterious. It didn't go any further that night, but he'd become smitten and looked forward to his next opportunity to walk her home.

JOE WAS WOKEN by youthful sounds in the morning. He opened his eyes to sunlight outside the window, and he could hear Joey bouncing in his crib, happily jabbering away. When he went into Joey's room, he was greeted by a big smile, more bouncing, and a ripe diaper.

After changing the diaper, Joe tickled Joey's ribs to rounds of giggles and laughter. Once dressed in a fleece onesie with feet, they went out to the kitchen, where he warmed a bottle, and sat in the living room rocking chair, feeding Joey. To Joe's delight, the little guy was much happier than the previous day. It wasn't long before they were joined by Katie, who came out of her room, carrying a small blanket and sucking her thumb.

When Joey had finished his bottle, Joe plopped him in the playpen and led Katie into the kitchen for breakfast. "Mom says you like cereal in the morning. Is that right?"

"Yes—Fruit Loops!"

With Katie in a booster seat, enjoying her cereal, Joe made himself a cup of coffee and sat alongside his daughter, watching her eat while mentally preparing for the day. Within minutes, his phone rang. He recognized the number. Checking the time, he saw it was just after eight o'clock.

"Good morning, Seth."

"Not so good, Joe. It seems they removed all the detainees overnight and refuse to say where they were taken."

Joe's shoulders sank, he slumped in the chair, and exclaimed, "Shit! No hearing?"

"No hearing. I just spoke to the Judge, and he's livid. We'll be having a conference call with the other attorneys at 9:00 to see where we go from here. I can tell you this is highly unusual and completely against the law. They're being denied due process."

As his anger built, Joe asked, "What can I do?"

"Just sit tight. I'll be in touch as soon as I know anything."

# CHAPTER 4

Mia and I had finished breakfast; she was working in her home office, and I was preparing to leave for work. I'm a private investigator, formerly a detective with the NYPD. While in the car, heading to an office I shared with my partner, Jim Abbott, my phone buzzed.

"Dan Burnett," I answered.

"Hi, Dan. Seth Bodner calling."

"Hey, man. How are things?"

"Might you be available to meet in my office this morning?"

"You sound serious, Seth. I'm just leaving Mamaroneck and can head your way now."

"That would be great. About a half hour?"

"Yup, see you then."

After turning onto the Rt. 287 entrance ramp toward White Plains, I recalled the work I'd done with Seth over the last year or so. The most recent was taking down a group of rogue cops from White Plains. It got hairy when they kidnapped my daughter, Hannah, from her college campus. Jim and I, along with two other buddies, rescued her in a military style raid that left two of the cops dead. Those were some of the worst days of my life. I hoped what Seth wanted to see me about would be nowhere near that intense.

Paula rose from her desk when I entered the office. "Good to see you, Dan."

Having recently helped celebrate her birthday, I knew Paula was fifty, married with children, and was an exceptional legal assistant. She took care of herself and dressed well.

"How've you been, Paula?"

"I can't complain. Seth is expecting you." Paula opened the door to the inner office.

"Thanks for coming," Seth said, gesturing for me to sit.

"No problem. What's up?" I asked, as always, struck by Seth's youthful appearance. Although I knew he was in his thirties, he looked like he was still in college, with straight blond bangs that bobbed when his head moved, and no indication that he'd ever needed to shave.

"You may not be aware of this, but I do pro bono work for many of the local religious organizations," Seth began. "On Sunday, ICE rounded up a dozen Muslims at a family festival in Ardsley. After an interview at the local police station, those who could prove they were US citizens were released. The rest were taken overnight to the Orange County Correctional Facility. A hearing was scheduled for this morning with an Immigration Judge, but sometime overnight, they were all removed from the facility and taken to an unknown location."

"Sounds like the doings of our new Department of Homeland Security."

"Exactly. Another Muslim group was targeted yesterday in Virginia."

"Wonderful," I said sarcastically. "How can I help?"

"We need to find out where they're being held, so their cases can be heard before they're all deported to only God knows where."

I let out an audible rush of air and said, "Where would we even start to look for them?"

"I have no idea, that's why I called you. A few other attorneys and I had a conference call with the Immigration judge an hour ago. We're supposed to come up with some ideas before another call at 1:00 this afternoon."

"Well, I guess we could start with known deportation staging areas. Maybe in Florida or Texas," I suggested.

"Okay, I believe the people being sent to El Salvador are flown out of Texas."

"Do we know anyone in Texas?"

"I don't. I could try to find a cooperative colleague down there who's not afraid of pissing off Washington."

"Let's try to determine from news stories what airports the deportation flights originated from. We can start there."

"Good idea. Paula can help with that. I've also been in touch with Congressman Latimer. He's trying to find out where they're being held."

"Or maybe he knows some elected Democrats in those states who are willing to assist."

"I'll call him back," Seth offered.

"Once we know where to look, I might be able to find a PI there who'll work with us."

Seth picked up the phone, buzzed Paula, and asked, "Can you look into news stories from the past few months and see where the immigrants who were flown out of the country left from?"... "Good. Before you do that, get me Congressman Latimer again, please."

While Seth waited for the call to go through, I said, "All right, I'll help Paula get started while you're on the call."

"Great. Thanks, Dan."

In the outer office, I sat with Paula while we googled: "News about deportation flights." I was using my phone while Paula typed on her Mac. It took us no time to determine that most flights departed from Harlingen, Texas, located in the southeast corner of the state. We also found a story that Avelo Airlines has recently been operating deportation flights from various Florida airports, as well as Mesa Gateway Airport in Arizona. While Paula typed up a list, I called my partner.

"Hey, Jim. Is there a directory of PIs in other areas of the country?"

"For sure, I have a printed copy in the office, but you can get it online. It's called the Investigator's Directory."

"Duh—that's too easy. Now I feel dumb for not trying that on my own."

"No worries," Jim laughed.

"Thanks, buddy."

As Paula finished her list of airports, I asked her to go to the Investigator's Directory website and print out a list for the same cities. Soon, we had information that I didn't even know existed a few minutes ago. I asked her to search for detention facilities in the same areas. Constantly amazed by current technology, I thought about how different my thirty years with the NYPD would have been if the internet had been around from the beginning.

When Seth had finished his call, he stepped out of his office and said, "The congressman wants to help, but it might be tomorrow before he has any information."

Paula handed him the lists, and he perused the printouts, smiled, and said, "Remind me to give you a raise!"

"I'll add that to your calendar," she laughed before resuming her work.

Once Seth and I had returned to his inner office, we debated how to proceed with the new information. I said, "My initial thought was to hire these PIs to assist, but if they're MAGA, it could work against us. If that's the route you want to go, I'll need some time to research their backgrounds."

"You're right, those are the most MAGA districts in the country. See how far you get today. I have that conference call with the judge in a few minutes. We'll touch base later this afternoon."

"You got it, Seth. Good luck!"

After getting a copy of the printouts from Paula, I drove to my office in Scarsdale. Along the way, I thought about the dramatic changes to our government over the last few months. Every night on TV, we saw people being rounded up by ICE, and we watched as they were imprisoned in El Salvador. While pretty much everyone agreed that we shouldn't let immigrants just stream across the Mexican border, and we all think criminals and gang members should be deported, the new administration was separating families again. Something they did in their first term, to the overwhelming objection of most Americans. It was something only the most heartless among us supported.

Jim was at his desk when I arrived, with CNN on the TV. "Good afternoon, Dan. I assume you want the Directory?"

"Yup. I was able to get most of what I needed online, but came in to do some background research on the PIs."

I told Jim about what I was working on and why I needed to do the research. He said, "I saw something on the news about that. The Feds whisked them out of state before the hearing?"

"Exactly."

"So it's Muslims this week? Last week, it was Venezuelans."

"I guess so. I'm hoping I can at least find out if any of these PIs are registered with a political party."

"I'll bet you can."

When I searched for a federal voter database online, I was directed to individual state websites. Starting with Texas, I discovered I'd need their birth dates to go along with their names. Fortunately, that information was listed in the directory I had in front of me. With a dozen PIs on my list in Texas, it took some time to pair the dates with the names, but it was doable. Out of those dozen names, six were registered Republicans, four were unaffiliated, and two were registered Democrats. I sent emails to the two Democrats.

Next, I tried Florida and found a roughly similar ratio for the fifteen PIs on my list, so I emailed four of them. In Arizona, the ratio was fifty-fifty, and I sent emails to two of them. It was now just a matter of time until I got replies.

While waiting, I made a list of what I'd be looking for. First up was whether they had any knowledge of the deportation staging locations, and if so, whether there had been any activity over the last twenty-four hours. Beyond that, I'd just need to gauge their level of interest and competence. I realized that if I were to engage someone, I'd need a list of people we were looking for, so I called Seth's office once again.

"Hi, Paula. Might you have a list of the detainees we're looking for?"

"Sure. I'll send it right over."

"Great. Did anything come out of Seth's call with the judge?"

"I'm not sure—I'll put him on."

A moment later, I heard, "Hey, Dan. How did you make out with the PIs?"

"I emailed a few I felt were safe. What did the judge have to say?"

"The judge has run it up the chain to the appeals court, but he thinks any inquiry with the DOJ or Homeland Security will just end up in the MAGA-verse. None of the other attorneys had any better ideas than what you and I came up with."

"Any word from Congressman Latimer?"

"Not yet, but if he comes up with any contacts in those states, maybe they can help vet the PIs."

"Good. Paula is sending me a list of the detainees. Might we be able to get pictures?"

"I would think so. I'll be speaking with one of their husbands later today. Shall I have him contact you directly?"

"Sure—I always like to get a feeling for the people involved."

With nothing left to do at the office, I gathered my notes to leave, but felt remiss for not keeping up with our other cases. I asked, "So what do you have cookin' this week, Jim?"

"Another divorce investigation—the wife wants to make sure the husband isn't gettin' jiggy with the financial statement."

"Any more collector car research requests?"

"Only one this week. Things seem to be slowing down with car collectors."

"It'll probably pick up before the next major auction."

"Yeah, let's hope."

**AFTER EXITING THE** parking lot and heading for Mamaroneck, my phone buzzed. "Dan Burnett," I answered.

"Hi, Dan, this is Joe Wilkinson. Seth Bodner asked me to call you."

"Yes, Joe. Your wife was picked up in the ICE raid?"

"That's right. We don't know where she is."

"I'd like to get a picture of her. What's your address? Maybe I can stop by your house."

"I'm in New Rochelle, 819 Wassermann Way."

"I know where that is, I lived in New Ro for twenty years."

"When are you thinking?"

"I'm on the road now, I can be there in twenty minutes or so, if that works for you."

"Great. I look forward to meeting you."

Rush hour traffic was brutal, as always. But as I made my way through town, a bunch of memories came flooding back. When passing by the old neighborhood, where my ex, Sheila, and I raised

Hannah, I pictured our daughter playing soccer with her friends in the yard. When I passed by Iona University, Hannah's alma mater, some of the worst days of my life flashed through my head. It was from this campus that she'd been kidnapped just a year ago—another case where someone was unexpectedly snatched away from a place they felt safe.

I ARRIVED AT Joe's house several minutes later. It was a modest home, a typical three-bedroom ranch in a neighborhood of similar post-World War II homes. After parking my Jeep Cherokee in the driveway, I was greeted by a tall, fit man in a tracksuit when I reached the door. He had a military crewcut and piercing blue eyes.

"Mr. Burnett, I assume?" he said, thrusting out his right hand.

"Yes, and please, it's Dan."

"Thanks for stopping by," he said as we shook hands. "Your timing is good; my toddler is napping." He gestured for me to follow him inside, where his young daughter was watching cartoons and drawing in a coloring book.

"Sorry to hear about your wife," I said. "This immigration thing has gotten out of hand."

"It certainly has. I'm in shock, actually. I'm sure she would have been released if there had been a hearing this morning."

"Tell me about how she came to this country."

After we were both seated, he turned down the television volume and said, "To make a long story short, until yesterday, I was in the Air Force. I met Ariana in Afghanistan—she was an interpreter and adviser at Bagram Airbase. We were married before the war ended, and I knew we'd need to get her out of there before we left. We did everything by the book and got her on a flight two weeks before the rest of us pulled out. It was a pretty hectic time, and we tried to get as many of our allies out of the country before the Taliban regained control."

"Yeah, I remember seeing it on TV."

"She had a special immigrant visa and was pregnant with Katie at the time." He nodded at his daughter. "After ninety days, Ariana received her Green Card, making her a permanent resident, and Katie was born four months later. She's a US citizen, along with our son, Joe Jr."

"Seth and I are determined to find your wife and get her in front of a judge. From what you've told me, she never should have been detained."

"What really pisses me off is that she's as much a war hero as any of us in uniform. I mean, she not only put her life at risk, but the lives of her family as well. She has an appointment next month to become a US citizen."

Hearing this confirmed how fucked up our country had become. "I get it, and I agree," I said, imagining how frustrated I would be if it were my family. "Can I get a picture or two of her?"

"Well, you can take the one next to you on the end table, or I can text you some from my phone."

"A text would be best, that way I can forward them."

"How many would you like?"

"Two or three recent photos from different angles."

"Sure. I have dozens."

"Great. Again, I'm sorry you and your children are going through this. It's not right."

As I rose to leave, he walked me to the door. "Thanks for coming by, Dan."

"You'll hear from Seth or me soon."

Once in the car, I texted Mia with my ETA. By the time I reached the end of the street, a text came in from Joe with the photos of Ariana.

# CHAPTER 5

It was a few minutes after 5:00 when I arrived at Mia's waterfront home in Mamaroneck. Entering through the garage, I heard her holler from her office that she was just wrapping up. I stepped into the kitchen and shook up a batch of Manhattans for our daily late afternoon cocktail.

By the time I'd strained them into martini glasses and dropped in the burgundy cherries, Mia came alongside, went up on her toes, and kissed me. At forty-eight, she's eight years younger than I, and still takes my breath away every time I see her. With long, dark hair cascading over her shoulders, framing hazel eyes with glints of gold, she radiated a natural beauty. Her commitment to yoga had kept her body lean, youthful, and alluring.

"How was your day, love?" she asked.

"Let's sit in the other room, and I'll tell you all about it."

We took our drinks around the corner into the living room and sat on the sofa before a wall of glass doors overlooking Long Island Sound. Our "happy place", where we usually enjoy our afternoon cocktail. It's also where we shared our first kiss a year and a half ago. I told Mia about my morning call from Seth, the ICE raid in Ardsley, and my meeting with Joe Wilkinson.

"I saw that story on the news—people have been protesting at Pascone Park all day. How is it that you always get involved with the headline stories that go viral?" Mia quizzed in disbelief.

"I have no idea, sweetheart. They just seem to find me."

Mia ran her fingers through my thick brown hair and smiled before kissing my cheek. She was sitting on her legs—with my tall, lanky frame, it was the only way we could make eye contact. Or lip contact, for that matter.

"This immigration thing is getting crazy. According to the news reports, some of the people were United States citizens," Mia said.

"That's true. They're definitely not violent gang members, and they're being denied due process. In all my years with the NYPD, I'd never heard of anything like it—the laws are crystal clear."

"I've also heard they're threatening to send the military into California to break up the protests out there, and they've reintroduced a travel ban from all the Islamic countries."

"That might explain why they're going after Muslims. Some of Seth's clients are from Afghanistan," I added.

"You know, we're all orbiting the sun together on this tiny blue ball. We should be trying to get along, not hating one another."

I smiled and pulled her close. Sometimes Mia could get philosophical and cut directly to the heart of the matter—and I loved her for it. "You're right, sweetheart."

After nursing our drinks for a few moments, she said, "I bought some fresh halibut for dinner tonight. How does that sound?"

"Wonderful. You know I love everything you make."

Mia and her former husband were foodies and had vacationed at famous European cooking schools while he was alive. When we'd finished our cocktails, she went into the kitchen to start dinner while I went upstairs to shower. When I returned, the table was set, and the fish was sizzling in a pan.

"Would you open a bottle of white, love? We've got about two minutes."

I opened the wine fridge and selected a bottle of Pinot Gris from Washington State, one of our favorites. By the time I'd opened it and poured us each a glass, she had set the plates on the table in a bay window with the same view as the living room. On each plate was a halibut fillet, seared to a light golden brown, nestled on top of steamed asparagus spears, and drizzled with a lemon Beurre Blanc sauce. My mouth watered at the sight of it as we sat down to eat.

After the first bite, I exclaimed, "Amazing, sweetheart! You've spoiled me for regular food."

"You know that's my intent," she replied with a grin.

"So tell me about your day."

"I spent the day sketching. We have a new client who's looking for a special dress for a holiday ball. I'm finding it a challenge to have it drape the way I want, using seasonal fabrics. Spring and summer fashions are easier to work with."

"I'm sure she'll love whatever you come up with—they always do."

"That's only because I'm obsessive," Mia laughed.

We'd finished dinner, cleared the table, and taken what was left of the wine to our happy place. Night had fallen, and we gazed out at the lights on Long Island, something we never seemed to tire of.

When our glasses were empty, Mia said, "I'm going up to bathe. Shall we go to bed early tonight?" She smiled, offering her lips. Her kiss left little doubt of what she had in mind for the evening.

WITH THE SUN peeking through the curtains, I awoke to an empty bed. Once I'd gone through my morning routine and dressed for the day, I could smell coffee while making my way down the stairs. At the bottom, to the right, I found Mia in her office, thumbing through swatch books.

"Good morning, lover," she said when she saw me in the doorway.

"Good morning. I see you woke up with some ideas?"

"Yeah. You know how it is." She smiled.

"That I do," I replied before heading for the kitchen. After my first sip of coffee, I scrolled through my messages. There were a few return emails from the PIs I had contacted, and a text from Seth that simply read: *Call me.*

I did just that.

"Hey, Dan. I just heard from Congressman Latimer. He's already reached out to colleagues in both Texas and Florida, and they're looking into any incoming immigrant flights over the last two days. He shared his colleague's contact info with me, in case there's anything specific we want to know."

"I'd like to vet some more of these PIs."

"Okay, send me their info and I'll forward it to them."

"You'll have it in five minutes. I met Joe Wilkinson yesterday, by the way."

"Colonel Wilkinson."

"Really? I knew he was in the Air Force, but he didn't state his rank."

"Yeah, he's a pretty modest guy. I'm glad he got his kids back before they were shipped out of state."

"He told me his wife is a legal permanent resident."

"She is."

"Then what in hell is going on?"

"Don't get me started, Dan. These assholes in Washington have lost their minds. They somehow think they have a mandate from the voters, giving them the right to disregard the law."

"They think 49.8% of the vote is a mandate?"

"You're preaching to the choir, Dan. They've lost every lawsuit so far, yet they keep trying to get away with this shit."

"Okay, I'll get the list of PIs over to you. What kind of budget do we have to work with?"

"Well, it's all pro bono work, so let's try to keep it to ten grand, at least for now. Send Paula one of your retainer contracts, and I'll get it right back to you."

"All right, I'll engage the PIs I feel comfortable with."

"Good. The clock is ticking—we want to locate these people while they're still in the country."

"Got it."

Once I'd sent the emails, I poured myself another coffee and reviewed the list. Due to the differences in time zones, I began with the ones in Florida. First on my list was Hal Baker, from West Palm Beach. He picked up on the first ring.

"Good morning, Hal. This is Dan Burnett calling. I'm a PI up in Westchester County, New York."

"Yes, Dan. I got your message yesterday. What can I do for you?"

"We have some Muslim members of our community who've been detained by ICE and covertly taken out of state. We're trying to find out if they've been taken to Florida."

"Do you know where?"

"No. We're not even sure it's Florida. We're also looking in Texas, and maybe Arizona. We'd like to locate them before they're deported."

"Well, you're looking in the right states. I know one airline has been doing deportation flights out of PBI. Let me look into recent activity at possible detention sites. I won't bill you unless I think I can help."

"That's more than fair, Hal. I appreciate it."

"You'll hear from me either way this afternoon."

"Great, thanks."

The next one up was Alberto Gonzales. While he sounded competent, he wanted to be on the clock at $90 an hour right away. I explained that I'd need to get approval from the attorney, and would call him back when I did.

I called the last of the Florida PIs to respond to my inquiry, and once I told him who we were looking for, he exclaimed, "I hope they rot in hell!" and hung up. As I suspected, some people still hold the entire Islamic faith responsible for 9/11.

Both of the PIs I contacted in Texas replied to my inquiry. It was after 9:00 there, so I called the first one, Daryl Munson.

"Munson Investigations," he answered. It sounded like he was driving and had me on speaker.

"Good morning, this is Dan Burnett—I emailed you yesterday."

"Yes, Dan. What can I do for you?"

"What do you know about deportation flights in Texas?"

"I know some leave from Harlingen, but I've also heard they've been flying out of Houston, El Paso, and the military base near San Antonio."

"Are there prisons around those places where the detainees are being held?"

"There're a dozen or so all over the state, both public and private. I'm not sure which ones feed which airports."

"We're looking for some Muslims from New York, a half dozen of them."

"I'll need more to go on than that. Texas is a big state."

Chuckling, I replied, "I know."

"If you can give me a clue where to start, I'd be happy to look into it."

"All we know is they left New York early Tuesday morning."

"Let me see if I can access any flight logs. I'll get back to you one way or the other."

"Thanks, Daryl. I appreciate it."

My call to the other Texas PI went to voicemail. My message simply asked for a return call.

While waiting for it to be after 9:00 in Arizona, I received an email from Seth. Along with the signed retainer, there were responses from Congressman Latimer's colleagues with PI recommendations. For Texas, there was a PI in Austin by the name of Bobby Lee, who came highly recommended.

In Florida, the recommended PI was the same Hal Baker that I'd already spoken to. With this additional endorsement, I felt confident about using Hal in Florida, but Texas was still up in the air. I entered Bobby Lee's number into my phone.

"The sleuth with the truth!" was how he answered.

"Mr. Lee?"

"Yes, this is Bobby Lee."

"This is Dan Burnett calling. I'm a PI up in New York. You were recommended by Congresswoman Crockett."

"I'm happy to hear she still remembers me. How can I help you?"

"I'm looking for some immigrants who may have been sent from New York to Texas in the last two days."

"Where in Texas?"

"We have no idea. That's why I'm calling."

"You think they were sent here in advance of being deported?"

"Exactly. Might you have any idea where to start?"

"Well, I know a couple of places that held the last few batches of immigrants before they were flown to El Salvador and Honduras."

"The people we're looking for are Muslims, both male and female, along with a child. Seven people in total."

"You said in the last few days?

"Two, to be precise."

"All right, let me do my thing, and I'll get back to you later today."

"Thanks. I appreciate it."

I felt good about finding help in Texas. Bobby might have been a bit cavalier, but he sounded both competent and confident, which I liked. I consulted a map of Arizona for Mesa Gateway Airport, and found it just east of Phoenix. With both of the PIs I contacted located in Phoenix, I tried Paul Grissom first.

"Grissom Investigations. This is Paul, " he answered.

After his professional greeting, I introduced myself and went through my spiel, explaining who I was looking for.

"Well, Dan, there have been hundreds of ICE Air deportation flights out of Mesa Gateway over the last several years. Most recently, they've been chartering flights from Avelo Airlines. I'm assuming you'd like to locate your people before they're deported?"

"Definitely. Most of them are documented and in the States legally."

"I hear that all the time."

"In this case, I know it to be true. Are they all held at the same location, pending deportation?"

"No. There are numerous facilities throughout the state. Let me put out some feelers for any recent incoming Muslims from New York. They might stand out because of their rarity out here. If I get any positive responses, I'll let you know."

"Thanks, Paul. I appreciate it."

My second call to Arizona was to Renaldo Alvarez. After telling him about who I was looking for, he said, "All the people who are deported from Arizona are Central Americans, and they're usually returned to their home countries. I doubt that they'd send Arabs to Mexico or Honduras."

Choosing not to correct him that all Muslims are not from Arabia, his point made sense; it was the first time I'd considered ICE doing something sensible. I thanked Renaldo for his time and ended the call.

It was nearing noon, and so far, I had nothing to show for my efforts. I thought about Joe Wilkinson and assumed he was climbing the walls by now. I considered calling him, but decided to leave it to Seth. Even though I'd done family counseling training while with the NYPD, I should be doing what I was hired to do: investigating.

# CHAPTER 6

Ariana hadn't slept since she was hustled out of her police station cell in the middle of the night. Still wearing handcuffs and shackles, she was led to a room where she joined the others from the festival at Pascone Park. There were seven remaining, including Ariana—two men, four women, and Mariam, a five-year-old girl who was friends with Katie.

They were led outside in the dark to a waiting van with nothing but the clothes on their backs. Once seated, they were each handed a packaged breakfast bar and a bottle of water. From her seat, Ariana could see the dashboard clock—it read 4:00. With three armed guards aboard, one of them driving, the van rumbled to life and followed the narrow road out through the gate and onto public roads.

This was not the way she had imagined this day to start. Seth Bodner, the attorney, told Ariana that she would see her family at a hearing today. He'd assured her that she'd be going home with them.

When the man seated next to her asked a guard where they were going, he was struck in the head with the butt of a shotgun by the guard in the front passenger seat. Ariana had grown up witnessing this sort of violence from authorities in Afghanistan—definitely not what she expected in the United States of America. No one spoke the rest of the way.

A half hour later, the van entered an unfamiliar airport and pulled alongside a commuter airline jet. Led by a guard onto the plane, Ariana was placed in a window seat and told to buckle her seatbelt before the next passenger was led aboard. It was the man who'd been struck, and she could see blood on the left side of his forehead. With each of them seated alone in a row, still cuffed and shackled, the engines started, the jet taxied to the runway, and took off into the ink black sky.

An hour later, as the eastern horizon began to brighten, Ariana tried to determine where they were going. So long as the morning sun remained on the left side of the aircraft, she knew they were heading south. Part of her training with the American military at Bagram was a course that taught basic survival skills and what they called "situational awareness"—skills she'd need if she were on the run from the enemy. She learned how to use the sun as a compass, how to listen effectively for sounds that went unnoticed by most people, and how to identify edible plant life and potable water, among other things.

At one point, she saw they were over the ocean, and Ariana feared they were being taken to Guantanamo Bay, the most dreaded place in the world. But soon they were again over land, and she recognized the coast of Florida. Once passing what she thought was Cape Canaveral, they were ordered to pull down their window shades. Ariana assumed her captors didn't want them to be able to identify where they landed.

When they touched down, after what Ariana estimated to be a two-and-a-half-hour flight, the plane taxied for another few minutes before the engines shut down. Dragging their shackles, they were led down the folding steps inside a hangar to a small bus, where they were blindfolded and driven for an hour. Ariana thought they were heading south, or maybe southeast. Even with her eyes covered, she could sense that the sun's warmth was mainly on her left side. Without air conditioning on the bus, it was hot and humid, further confirming they were in Florida.

An hour later, they left the smooth roadway and traveled down a bumpy, unpaved road. While she couldn't see the dust, she could taste it. They were told to remove the blindfolds as they exited the bus at what appeared to be a concrete-walled prison. In the absence of any signs or markings on the building, the surrounding orange groves were the only means of identifying her location.

They were taken to one large cell with concrete walls on three sides and prison bars on the other. On one wall was a small window, too high to see anything but sky, although Ariana could at least determine the time of day.

There were eight flimsy folding beds in the room, four on each side, as well as a stainless steel toilet and sink in one corner, offering no privacy. The room reeked of mildew and bleach, and Ariana gagged on what came up from her stomach. On each bed was a blanket, a pillow, and a towel. When the cell door closed, everyone looked at one another, still afraid to speak. Having no idea how long they would be here, Ariana sat on the bed farthest from the toilet, claiming it as her own.

That was when depression began to set in. Up until then, she'd been focused on situational awareness, gleaning any bit of information available. But now she felt hopeless, fearing she'd never see her family again. As tears rolled down her cheeks, she began sobbing and buried her face in the pillow. When she had dispelled her tears, she knelt on top of the mattress and began to pray. She guessed it was late morning, not yet noon. She recited the Dhuhr prayer.

While she found peace, it was not everlasting. With no air conditioning, it became stiflingly hot as the day went on. Ariana joined in on the conversation with her cellmates, who had been sharing their stories about where they were from and how they'd come to America. The stories were similar in that each of them had escaped oppression, poverty, or war. Two of them had escaped from Iraq after their homes had been destroyed by bombs. American bombs.

Ariana formed a connection with Rihana, who had the bed next to hers. They both came from Afghanistan and had attended school, a rarity for young women. She and her family had been granted asylum in Great Britain, where she continued her education, which explained her British accent. At thirty years old, she was just a few years younger than Ariana.

"How did you come to America?" Ariana asked.

"In London, I worked for Bank of America. When an opening for a financial analyst position became available in New York, I applied and got the job. They arranged for my immigrant Visa, and within a year, I became a permanent resident."

"So, you're still a citizen of the UK?"

"Yes, and I have a UK passport. I'm so thankful that they granted my family asylum. I'll never give up my citizenship there."

Ariana told Rihana her story and about her children. Rihana said she always wanted children, but so far, she hadn't found the right husband.

Later that afternoon, they prayed together, this time the Asr prayer. As perspiration streamed down their faces, the two women longed for a fan.

At some point, Ariana heard the guards in the hallway. She heard the clinking of keys and the sounds of the barred doors opening and closing. She could also smell food, setting off pangs of hunger in her belly. By the time the guards reached their door, the anticipation of eating had consumed her. But when she saw what was on their trays, she recoiled in disgust. There was a bowl of soupy mashed potatoes topped with an unidentifiable brown meat and shiny gravy. What had initially smelled appetizing from a distance now reeked.

Using a plastic fork, Ariana tried a bit of it, but was unable to swallow. She made do with a piece of stale bread and an orange. *Thank God for the orange!* While not very filling, she savored each section one by one, noticing Rihana doing the same.

Once their trays were taken away, Ariana led the entire group in the evening prayer. Having no idea when the sun went down, they recited both the Maghreb and Isha prayers.

JOE WILKINSON HAD kept his head straight all morning by getting to know his children. After breakfast, with Joey in his lap and Katie sitting alongside on the sofa, Joe read to them. Katie picked the books; the first was Dr. Seuss' *Green Eggs and Ham.* While Katie seemed to know every word, Joey was fascinated by the colorful pictures and by the sound of his father's deep voice. A few pages in, the boy reached for Joe's lips and felt them move while he spoke.

At the conclusion of each book, Katie would select another for Joe to read. The last was *Coyote Sunrise,* which they only got halfway through before Joey began to fidget and fuss. Joe thought he might just be tired of holding still and placed Jr. in his playpen, but the fussing continued.

Katie said, "Maybe he needs a bottle, Daddy."

"Thanks, honey. You were right the last time—I'll give it a try."

Joe went into the kitchen and returned with a perfectly warmed bottle, plucked Joey from the crib, and held him while he drank from the bottle. Instantly content, he boy fell asleep when the bottle was mostly finished, and Joe carried him to his room, gently lowering him into his crib. Suspecting his diaper needed changing, Joe ignored it for the time being, unwilling to disturb the boy's sleep.

He returned to the living room to find Katie in front of the TV, watching cartoons, and realized how effective a babysitter the TV could be. He watched with her for a while, but by noon, he'd become impatient waiting to hear back from Seth Bodner. With Katie occupied and Joey asleep, he used the opportunity to call the attorney.

"Law offices," the same female voice answered.

"Joe Wilkinson calling. Is this Paula?"

"Yes, Colonel. Seth is on another line at the moment. Might I be able to help you?"

"Maybe. I'm anxious for any new information."

"Seth has been working the phones all morning, but I'm not aware of any new information. How are you holding up?"

"My toddler's kept me occupied all morning, but I'm anxious to know what's going on."

"I certainly understand—I'll have him get back to you as soon as he finishes this call."

"Thank you. I'll be standing by."

Again, Joe relied upon his "hurry up and wait" skills to remain calm, but could not shake the sense of a ticking clock. A few minutes later, Seth returned his call.

"I'm sorry, Colonel, but I have nothing new to report. We have at least three congressmen working on it, as well as private detectives in three states. We're focusing on the southern states where previous deportation flights originated. If we can find out where they're being held, we'll use the courts to put a stop to it."

"What possible legal justification would they have to deport Ariana?" Joe asked impatiently.

"Absolutely none. All of this is illegal—unconstitutional as a matter of fact."

"Is there anything I can do to help? I've spent the last decade in military intelligence."

"I can't think of anything at the moment, but I'm all ears if you have any ideas."

"All right, I'll let you know if I do."

"Do you still have Dan Burnett's number?"

"Yes. He left a card when he was here yesterday."

"If you can't reach me, feel free to call him with any ideas. He has more investigation experience than I do. Rest assured, Joe, you'll be the first to know if I learn anything."

"Okay, Seth. I appreciate the call back."

Joe returned to the living room and sat down to think. Perhaps the long-remembered sound of cartoons would open his mind to fresh ideas. With Katie snuggled against his arm, he began to imagine how the government would covertly deport someone. Joe was thoroughly familiar with covert operations and had run many of them himself while stationed overseas. The military excelled at keeping secrets, typically by limiting access to those with a need-to-know. It suddenly dawned on him that the people in Washington running this operation would likely utilize the military.

Joe had already learned which states the flights had originated, and thought they'd likely be from military airfields. As he recalled the airfields in those states, he thought he might know some of the officers there. He retrieved his laptop from the bedroom and went to work on the kitchen table with a yellow legal pad. Within a half hour, he had a list of the bases that had, or were near, an airfield.

Next, after logging into the secure Armed Forces personnel portal, he began searching for anyone he knew personally who was stationed at those bases. Joe jotted down the officers he knew at each of them. The entire time he was doing the research, he was thinking about what he hoped to accomplish by calling them, and what exactly he'd say. When he had a few names at the bases that he felt comfortable contacting, he began making calls.

The officer he knew best was at the air station in Corpus Christie, Texas. He asked the switchboard operator for Major J.T. Willis, with whom Joe flew air-to-air refueling missions a few years ago.

"Major Willis."

"Hi, J.T., Joe Wilkinson calling."

"Hello, Colonel. Good to hear from you. Is it true that you pulled the plug?"

"Yup. I completed my twenty years three days ago."

"How does it feel to be out?"

"I don't know yet. Excuse me for getting right to the point, but my wife was just picked up by ICE and transported out of state. Given your location, I'm hoping you're familiar with the deportation flights."

"Oh my God, that's terrible, Joe. How can I help?"

"I assume the immigrants are held somewhere awaiting deportation. I'm trying to locate her while she's still in the States."

"She's an immigrant?"

"Yes, from Afghanistan, one of the translators and informants we worked with during the war. I brought her home with me three years ago, all by the book. She's a legal resident, and we have two children born in this country."

"Sounds like another government snafu, Joe. I wish I knew where to start; can you give me more to go on?"

"She's among a group of seven Muslims from New York. They most likely arrived this morning, but I don't know where."

"All right, I'll see what I can find out. What's her name?"

"Ariana. Ariana Wilkinson. Thirty-two years old, 5'1", about 110 pounds with dark hair."

"I'm on it, Colonel."

"Thanks, Major."

"Oh, congratulations on becoming a father!"


**HAPPY TO HAVE** made a helpful connection on his first call, Joe sat back, wondering what to do next. A moment later, he heard his son bouncing in the crib. When he went into Joey's room, Joe found a happy boy, despite again needing a diaper change.

According to Ariana's list of instructions, it was time for Joey to be fed baby food in his highchair. Initially, Joe assumed his son could feed himself. But after serving it to him in a bowl, he quickly discovered that Joey could not find his own mouth with the spoon. However, he did enjoy flinging the food around the kitchen, laughing the whole time. Suppressing his own laugh, and with Katie's help, they managed to get Joey fed without creating too much of a mess.

Having accomplished that, and with Joey back in his playpen, Joe made tomato soup with peanut butter and jelly sandwiches for him and Katie. Finding out for himself the extent of work involved with caring for children, Joe wondered when he'd find the time to make the rest of his phone calls. It might have to wait until Jr. was asleep for the night. Yet he still felt the sense of a ticking clock. Every minute that passed increased the possibility that Ariana would be shipped out of the country, to only God knew where.

While on the floor, playing with Joey and his toy cars, Joe's phone rang.

"Good afternoon, Joe. Dan Burnett calling."

"Good to hear from you—any progress?"

"No new information yet, but I have some PIs in Florida and Texas looking for your wife. How are you holding up?"

"In all honesty, the kids are keeping me busy, but after speaking with Seth, I've been calling friends at military airfields in Texas. I'm hoping they can determine where ICE holds people before flying them out of the country."

"Great idea. Any luck so far?"

"Not yet, but there are a few high-ranking officers with staff working on it."

"Good. Seth has some people in Congress looking for them, along with a few of his attorney friends in Florida and Texas. Between the three of us, we might catch a break."

"I hope sooner, rather than later," Joe declared.

"Me too. As Seth would say, 'Time is of the essence.'"

# CHAPTER 7

By mid-afternoon, I'd still not heard anything from my fellow PIs. While there was still time left in the day, I was becoming anxious. As I attempted to organize my notes and lists, I received a call from Seth. "Any news?" I asked.

"Nothing useful. Besides the congresspeople in Florida and Texas, I reached out to some lawyer friends I have down there. They're calling around."

"I still haven't heard back from my PI associates, but I expect to get some reports by the end of the day."

"Do me a favor: call Colonel Wilkinson for me. He's probably going crazy by now stuck at home with his kids. I'm sure he's a take-charge guy and will want to know what's going on. I've already disappointed him once today. Perhaps you could brief him on your efforts."

"As a matter of fact, I just did. He has some military contacts who've joined the search."

"Good to hear."

"I'll keep him up to speed."

Glancing at the time on the computer screen, I saw it was 3:00, and I hadn't yet eaten lunch. I didn't recall Mia having lunch either, so I rose from the dining room table and looked in on her. She seemed just as focused on her work as I was. There were sketches taped to the walls, and fabric swatches strewn about her office. She was standing in front of her desk, facing away from me, pairing fabrics together in groupings. Fearful of startling her, I tapped lightly on the door until she saw me. Turning, she smiled and motioned me closer with open arms. We hugged one another, before she turned her head to kiss me.

After the kiss, I asked, "Are you working straight through?"

"I wasn't planning on it, but the time just got away from me."

"Me, too. Shall we just hold off for dinner?"

"Maybe. I'd like to get the fabrics selected before calling it a day."

"Okay, I'll just grab an apple. I'm still expecting some calls."

"Cocktail hour at 5:00?"

"Perfect!"

With an apple and a can of Diet Coke, I returned to my seat in the dining room and continued organizing my lists. My phone rang, and I saw a Florida area code.

"This is Dan."

"Hi, Dan. Hal Baker calling."

"Yes, Hal. What did you find out?"

"I discovered an old acquaintance who works for the Department of Corrections. He knows which facilities ICE uses to house the immigrants and which airports are being used. While he's not assigned to immigrants, he knows some people who are. I might be able to help you after all."

"Great! Email me one of your terms of engagement, and we'll get you on the clock."

After sharing my email address, I added, "I'll include a list of names, and anything else you might find helpful."

"All right, you'll have my contract in a moment."

Feeling like I caught a break in Florida, I put together some information I thought Hal would find useful and sent it off with his signed contract.

A few minutes later, I heard back from Bobby Lee in Austin. "Hi, Dan. Sorry, it took me so long to get back to you, but I just wrapped up a cheating wife case—photos and everything! It should pay the bills for a while."

"Paying the bills is always a good thing," I chuckled.

"You got that right. Anyhow, regarding the immigrant flights. Just about all of them leave from the southeast corner of the State, between Houston, Corpus Christi, and San Antonio. There's an airport in Harlingen that seems to be the main departure point. Most of the immigrants who were sent to El Salvador left from there, and before leaving, were housed at East Hildago Correctional—the place is run by ICE."

"You've had a productive day, Bobby. Do you see a path forward to find the people we're looking for?"

"Maybe. I don't have any contacts down there, so I'll have to take a ride and poke around a bit. It's about a five-hour drive."

"All right, we can swing that. Send me a terms of engagement contract and I'll get it right back to you."

"Good, I'll head down there in the morning."

"Thanks, Bobby."

I received his contract a few minutes later and returned it with the same information I'd sent to Hal.

It was nearing 5:00, and I'd still not heard from Daryl Munson, the other PI I'd spoken to in Texas. Running out of patience, I called him again.

"Hi, Dan. I was just about to call you."

"No worries, Daryl. I know it's an hour earlier there."

"I had no luck accessing flight logs. That information seems to be closed to the public, and I have no contacts in Air Traffic Control. I'll need more to go on before I can help you."

"All right. Your mention of Air Traffic Control gives me an Idea. If I learn anything, I'll get back to you."

"Fair enough, Dan. Good luck with it."

Wondering if Colonel Wilkinson's military contacts might be able to access the air logs, I called him next.

"Hi, Joe. Here's what I've got for you: We've hired a private investigator in Florida who has a friend in the Corrections Department. He thinks he might be able to find out the comings and goings at the facilities down there."

"Good!" I could hear the relief in his voice that progress was being made.

"We also have a PI in Texas, who's heading to Harlingen in the morning to see what he can find out."

"Also good to hear."

"There might be something else you can help with."

"Talk to me."

"Can your military contacts can get their hands on flight logs for the state of Texas?"

"Maybe. I'll find out. I assume we're looking for inbound flights arriving this morning?"

"Precisely."

"All right. I'm all over it."

"Great. Have a good evening, Joe."

I closed up my laptop and plugged it in to recharge before heading to the kitchen to make cocktails. When Mia heard the shaker, she joined me.

"Cosmopolitans?" she asked.

"That's the only pink drink I know," I grinned.

After we each took a sip, I heard "Mmm," just before she kissed me. Sharing the taste in our mouths, the kiss became serious, until we were afraid of spilling our drinks.

"Let's take these to our happy place, love."

"After you."

Once seated, Mia said, "I overheard some of your conversations today. Are you making any progress locating the Muslims?"

"Nothing specific yet, but we've got a bunch of irons in the fire. We're now just waiting for something to break."

"You sound hopeful."

"Yeah, maybe I am." I told her about the PIs I'd hired, our political contacts, and Joe's inside line on the airbases and flight information.

"Sounds like a full-court press!" she exclaimed.

"It's everything we could think of."

A moment later I asked, "Did you get your fabrics picked out?"

"I've narrowed it down to two pallets. I'll let the customer make the final decision."

"Good call, sweetheart."

"Are you up for grilling some filets tonight?"

"Definitely."

"Good. I'll make some Au Poivre sauce while you're grilling."

"There's a little more Cosmo left in the shaker. Do you want a top off?"

"Sure."

Dinner was marvelous, and afterward, we took what was left of a bottle of cabernet to our happy place and watched boat traffic on the sound—our evening ritual. With Mia sitting at one end of the sofa, I stretched out with my head on her lap, as she caressed my forehead. The next thing I knew, she was trying to wake me and help me up the stairs. I hoped I hadn't spoiled her plans for the evening.

**I WAS THE** first one up the next morning. I had a lot happening that day, and I wanted to get to it. As I sipped my coffee, I found myself drumming my fingers, feeling the pressure to locate Ariana before being shipped out. It was too early to make phone calls, so I began organizing my notes and lists into a three-ring binder. This was my lifelong method of managing an investigation. The more information I gathered, the more I needed to access it easily in chronological order—what I referred to as a case book. I'd call it a "murder book" if I were working a homicide.

With my work almost complete, I received a call from Joe Wilkinson.

"Am I calling too early, Dan?"

"Not at all, I've been up for an hour."

"I just got a call from Major Willis in Corpus Christi. He says there were no ICE flights into Texas yesterday morning between 0300 and 1200 hours, CST."

"All right, not to question him, but how would he identify an ICE flight?"

"ICE flights are required to file flight plans, and all their previous flights complied with that requirement. The plans include the takeoff and landing locations."

"What if they were trying to fly covertly?"

"Even if they weren't identifying it as an ICE flight, the altitude they're flying requires a flight plan."

"So no flights flew from New York to Texas yesterday morning?"

"Only commercial airlines and a few biz jets. And we know who owns the biz jets from their tail numbers."

"Okay, Joe, thanks for the explanation. What are your thoughts?"

"I think we can rule out Texas."

"Okay, we'll focus our attention elsewhere. Do you have any contacts in Florida?"

"As a matter of fact, I do. I reached out to a couple of them yesterday, but haven't heard back yet, and there's another guy I'm about to try. I'll let you know if I hear anything."

"Thanks, Joe."

I sent Seth an email explaining this latest development, then considered calling Bobby Lee to pull him off the case. However, after giving it some thought, I decided not to. I'd learned over the years to confirm information from multiple sources whenever possible, and Bobby would only cost us a day or two at $700 per.

Seth called a few minutes later to discuss my email. "So is Texas off the table?"

"Maybe. I still have a PI heading to Harlingen and should get a report from him later today. Colonel Wilkinson is in contact with some Air Force buddies in Florida. The hope is that they can access flight logs there, as they did in Texas."

"What are your thoughts on Arizona?"

"From what I can tell, they mainly deal with Central Americans in California, Arizona, and New Mexico. I'd find it unlikely ICE would fly them there all the way from New York. I'm not saying we rule it out, let's just put it on the back burner for now."

"Makes sense. So we focus on Florida?"

"That's my thinking."

"All right, keep in touch."

As soon as I hung up with Seth, Hal Baker called.

"Good morning, Dan."

"Hey, Hal. What do you have for me?"

"My guy at corrections gave me a full picture of the ICE detention facilities. There are four primary locations. One in Miami, one in Pompano, another in Moore Haven, which is just west of Lake Okeechobee, and one more in MacClenny, up near Jacksonville."

"Okay, where do we go from here?"

"My guy said he'd make some calls this morning to see if a group came in from New York yesterday. I'll need to wait to hear from him, unless you have any new information."

"None that would help you narrow it down, but we're focusing on Florida for sure. We received some flight log info early this morning indicating that it's unlikely they were taken to Texas."

"Interesting. How did you access the flight log information?"

"From a contact in the military."

"Can they get the same info from Florida?"

"Maybe. We're working on it," I said optimistically.

"All right. If I knew where they landed, I'd know the closest Detention Facility."

"You'll be among the first to know, Hal. I'll be in touch."

With a few pokers still in the fire, I went to the kitchen for breakfast. Mia had a fruit salad prepared in the fridge, so I sat in front of the TV with a bowl of fruit and another coffee, watching the news. It wasn't long until Mia appeared wearing yoga attire, glowing slightly with a towel around her neck.

"Good morning, love," she said.

"I didn't even know you were awake, sweetheart."

"Yeah, I don't make a lot of noise doing yoga," she teased.

"What do you have on the docket today?"

"I have a lunch meeting in the city today with my client. I'm hoping she likes my fabric selections."

"I wouldn't worry, they always do."

"Thanks for the confidence," she said as she kissed my forehead before heading up the stairs.

With this bit of exchange fresh in my mind, I was reminded of how much I loved this woman. We'd been together for a year and a half, and all our exchanges were just as sweet and caring as this one. I couldn't recall a cross word ever spoken between us. Besides her natural beauty, she was the most talented chef I'd ever known, and the sexiest woman on the planet. Not to mention independently wealthy. To this day, I didn't know what I ever did to deserve a woman like Mia.

A phone call brought me back down to earth. "Hey, Dan. Joe Wilkinson again."

"Yes, Colonel, what-cha got?"

"My guy in Texas is looking into Florida for us, and I'm thinking maybe we can track upcoming flights, too. That might give us a clue as to where there are people to transport."

"If you're looking for a post-retirement career, you'd make a great PI, Joe. That's another great idea. We need everything we can get."

"Good. I'm on it."

After the call ended, I tried to recall other cases where an amazing source of information came along with it. I couldn't think of any, not even in my thirty years with the NYPD.

I opened the case book again, out of habit. In actuality, I was impatient waiting for phone calls to come in.

The next was from Hal. "Okay, Dan, we may have something: My guy in corrections tells me a small group of Muslims arrived yesterday at the Glades County Corrections Facility. That's the prison in Moore Haven, near Lake Okeechobee."

With a fist pump, I said, "Bingo, that might be our people."

"I would think so. It's about an hour and twenty minutes' drive, so I'll head out there now. I'm not sure what I'll do when I get there, but I'll be close by if we need to move quickly."

"Good. Stay in touch today."

"You got it."

I called Seth, "We might have a lead. The PI in West Palm just got word that a small group of Muslims arrived at Glades County Jail yesterday."

"All right! Do we have a plan?"

"No plan yet. Hal's on his way there now to scope it out. We'll devise a plan when we have some more information. We first need to confirm that they're there. Who knows, maybe they have visitor hours," I chortled.

"Should we keep this between ourselves for the moment?" Seth asked.

"How do you mean?"

"I mean, should I let the Florida congressman know about this? Maybe he can confirm it somehow."

"Let me think about that. If word gets out that we know where they are, they might move them again. We need to be extremely cautious. At least for now."

"All right, I trust your instincts. But we should let the Colonel know."

"I'll do that right now."


JOE ANSWERED ON the first ring, "Hey, Dan."

"We might have caught a break, Joe." I told him about the latest development.

"Where exactly is Glades County Prison?"

"Moore Haven, just west of Lake Okeechobee."

"Give me a moment to locate that on a map."

Standing by while I heard some keyboard clicks, he quickly came back and said, "Ten minutes ago, I got some flight log data from Florida. There are a handful of inbound flights that fit our profile. I'm trying to reconcile if any of them landed near Okeechobee."

"I'll hold, take your time."

A few moments later, he said, "I know where most of the major cities are in Florida. It appears that West Palm Beach and Fort Myers would be the closest to Glades County."

"That sounds about right."

"Okay, I see no morning flights to Fort Myers, other than commercial, but there is one into PBI that originated in Teterboro, New Jersey. It landed at 10:00."

"That fits."

"And here's another originating in Newburgh, New York, that arrived in Sebring at 8:19."

"That also fits. Both of those airports are about an hour away from Glades County," I said.

"Yeah, I can see that on the map, but Newburgh is closer to Orange County, New York, and the timing seems to fit better if they left in the dark."

"We don't have any confirmation as to when they left, but it doesn't really matter. Either flight could have delivered them to Glades County."

"Agreed. Where do we go from here, Dan?"

"Let me share this with the PI down here. In the meantime, see what else you can find out about those flights. We'll touch base soon."

THINGS WERE STARTING to come together, and I felt the familiar rush of adrenaline that came over me when closing in on a target. I called Hal.

"Yo, Dan."

"I have flight log confirmation of two morning flights that could have delivered our people; one to PBI and another to Sebring."

"Good to know. That would confirm Glades County."

"Yeah, we're on the right track."

"How do you want me to handle it at the prison?"

"What if you go in as a visitor and ask to see a prisoner?"

"Let me check with my corrections guy if that's something doable. I'll get back to you in a bit."

When that call ended, I dialed Seth's number again.

"How are we making out, Dan?" After I filled him in on the latest events, he said, "All right, now that we've located them, what do we do?"

"Hal is looking into whether it's possible to go to the prison and ask to see a prisoner. What pitfalls do you see with that?"

"I wonder if they'll even acknowledge that they're there."

"Yeah, there's that."

"Let me speak with one of my attorney friends down there. I'll let you know what he says."

"All right, Seth."

My next incoming call was from Bobby Lee in Texas, "Good morning, Dan. Do you have a minute?"

"I do."

"All right, I made it to Harlingen airport yesterday and poked around a bit. I spoke to a few airport workers as they left for the day, and spent a few hours at a bar near the employees' parking lot last night. While trying not to be obvious, I struck up a couple of conversations and overheard a few others. It sounds like there's been no ICE activity in the last few days. Some people remarked at how quiet it's been."

"Good. I like how you handled that."

"I also learned about the location of the local ICE detention facility. I could go poke around out there this morning if you'd like."

"Yeah, spend another few hours and see what you can find out. Do you think they'd be open to a prisoner visit?"

"Maybe. Do you want to give me a name?"

I quickly scanned the detainee list for a male name. "Yeah, ask for Muhammad Bashire, and see how they react. If it looks like a dead end, head home this afternoon."

"Okay, Dan. I'll let you know."

# CHAPTER 8

Ariana woke to a skirmish in the cell. Two of the women, Layla and Farah, were arguing over a pillow. "Ladies!" Ariana admonished. "Is that in the spirit of Allah?"

They both froze, looking at their feet.

"Look, I know we're all afraid. Perhaps we should pray together."

"Yes, let's pray," said Muhammad, a house painter from Yonkers.

Below the buzzing fluorescent lights, Ariana again knelt on her mattress, now damp from the stifling Florida humidity. While she was among the youngest there, her voice carried a calmness of someone older and wiser. Of someone who remembered that God sees beyond borders and jail cell bars.

The others got on their knees, facing Ariana. On her right was Rihana, and across from her was Farah, who, along with her daughter, Mariam, was the only one wearing hijabs. Most of them led typical American lives, where a hijab would only draw attention to themselves.

Unable to determine the time of day, Ariana took a deep breath and recited an appropriate prayer: *"Bismillah ir-Rahman ir-Rahim...*" Her voice wove through verses of Sarah Al-Inshirah, "*Have we not expanded for you your chest...*"

Something changed in the oppressive air. Their heartache didn't vanish, but it became less encompassing. The sounds of distant guards and muffled sobs from the cell next door faded behind the cadence of ancient Arabic. As they continued, a guard appeared at the bars and shouted, "Quiet!

Halting their chants, they remained kneeling until the guard walked away; then, they continued their prayer in whispers. When Ariana finished, silence settled over them, not out of fear, but of surrender to Allah. He would take care of them.

Farah, with moist eyes, said softly, "They want us afraid." Looking from one face to the next, she hugged Mariam close. "But they can't take this. Not what's in here." She placed her hand on her heart. "We bend only to Allah."

Layla finally spoke—just one word, "*Ameen.*"

For the first time since their arrival, the group was at peace. The long silence was broken when Muhammad said, "What will become of us? Where will we be taken next?"

No one had an answer. But for now, they had this—the seven of them together, clinging to whatever fragments of dignity and hope they could muster. Somehow, with the help of Allah, that had to be enough.

**WHEN JOE WILKINSON** had finished feeding his children, he led them to the living room, where he again placed Joey in the playpen, while Katie watched cartoons.

He hated using the TV as a pacifier, something he swore he'd never do when he was away, longing to see them. But getting their mom back was imperative.

Joe had been up early and already spoken with J.T. Willis, who'd managed to access the flight logs for the states of Texas and Florida. Dan Burnett had also called with information that all but confirmed Ariana was in a Florida prison.

While Dan and Seth worked on a plan for getting Ariana and her friends out of there, Joe and J.T. focused on learning all they could about upcoming ICE flights. They knew the clock was ticking, but they didn't yet know how fast.

Again with J.C. on the phone, Joe asked, "How far in advance does ICE typically file their flight plans?"

"Not far. They usually file just before takeoff, and sometimes after they're in the air. I doubt we'll get much advance notice, other than their actual flight time."

"That's not much. We're looking for flights into PBI, RSW, or SEF, which is Sebring."

"Okay, Joe. You'll be the first to know if any of those destinations pop up in a flight plan."

"Thanks, buddy."

While waiting for the next shoe to drop, Joe played with his kids on the floor, wrestling and tickling. Jr. found great delight in watching Joe lie on his back and lift Katie in the air. In this position, she could pretend to fly like Wonder Woman, making a whooshing sound as she flew. When it was Joey's turn, he just giggled uncontrollably, not really getting the whole flying thing.

As Joe was enjoying the opportunity to play with the children, they were interrupted by a phone call. He recognized the number as Dan's.

"Hi, Joe. My Florida PI just walked into the Glades County Prison and asked to see one of the men from Ariana's group. He was told there was no one there by that name. Seth and I discussed it and determined that they're lying. And since there's no way we can bust them out like a John Wayne western, Seth has engaged a Florida attorney to file a Writ of Habeas Corpus. That should at least force them to acknowledge a prisoner's existence, laying the groundwork for release. The attorney will then request an emergency hearing with a judge to demonstrate why they're not subject to deportation. And even if a decision isn't made immediately, they should be allowed to post bond."

"That all sounds like good news. Am I missing something?" Joe asked.

"If this were occurring in New York, I would say no. But Florida is MAGA-land. They might not comply with a court order, at least not without a fight. Who knows if we can even get an honest judge to hear the case."

"Would it help if I came down there?"

"A grieving husband in uniform can only be a positive thing. Especially with all your ribbons and medals. But hold off until you hear from Seth."

"All right, although I'll start looking for someone to watch the kids if I have to come down."

"Good idea."

"Thanks, Dan."

**WISHING HE HAD** any nearby relatives, Joe wondered how to go about finding childcare. He didn't know any of Ariana's friends or whom he could trust. After considering who he knew locally, there was only Liz, the neighbor next door, who he'd spoken to for less than a minute. Joe thought Imam Khan at the Muslim Center would be his best bet and made the call.

"Westchester Muslim Center."

"Good morning. Joe Wilkinson calling for Imam Khan."

"Hold please."

A moment later, Joe heard, "Colonel, how are you today?"

"Fine, Imam. We may be getting close to locating my wife and your congregants."

"That's wonderful news. I've been sick to my stomach for two days. Can you share the information?"

Safeguarding what he knew, Joe replied, "We believe it's somewhere down south—we hope to narrow it down today. The reason for my call is if I have to go get her, I'll need someone to care for my children—we have no family in the area."

"That should be no problem. We have a daycare staff on site, and they already know Katie and Joey. "I'm sure one of the staff would love to take them for an overnight or two."

"That's great, I can't begin to tell you what a relief that is."

"Not a problem. Fatima Bilal runs the program—I'll make her aware of the situation. Just call here and ask for Fatima if you want some help."

"Thank you, Imam."

Relieved to have that issue solved, Joe looked into flight possibilities from White Plains to PBI. JetBlue had a half dozen daily non-stops, at all hours of the day.

**WITH THE NEW** information from Dan, Seth called Johnny Ziegler, his attorney friend in West Palm, whom he'd known since law school. They had spoken earlier, so Johnny was familiar with the situation. "Hey, buddy, we believe our group is being held at the Glades County Detention Center. We sent a PI in there an hour ago asking to visit one of them, but he was told there was no one there by that name."

"And you're pretty sure he, or she, was there?"

"Yeah, it was a he. We have two sources who believe they are there."

"Do you want me to file a Writ?"

"Can you find a non-MAGA judge?"

"Yeah, I know a few."

"Good—do it. I'll email you the names."

"I'll keep you posted."

Seth felt more in control, now that they were taking a legal path. Although he was well aware of the slow wheels of justice, it was a route he understood. After sending the names of each person in the Muslim group, Seth planned how they'd respond to the roadblocks they were likely to face. There was an abundance of case law for him to review, and thankfully, this was federal law, which wouldn't be subject to the quirky differences in state laws.

**AFTER HAL BAKER** struck out with the prisoner visit, he hung out across the street, hoping to watch the guards leave at the end of their shifts. He had no idea when that would be, but since he had nothing else to do, he decided to wait. Around 1:00, he noticed activity in the side parking lot, with some vehicles arriving, while others were departing. It appeared to be a changing of the guard.

In the middle of the outgoing procession was a pick-up, all jacked up for off-road use with monster knobby tires. There was a light bar on the roof with what appeared to be enough lights for a stadium, along with a push bar to protect the truck's grill. However, the most striking aspect of the truck, the reason it caught his attention, was the enormous flags mounted above the bed.

The flags were at least four feet high and six feet long, streaming in the air as the truck moved forward. The flag on the left read "HANDS OFF OUR GUNS", and the one on the right, "GO GATORS".

In addition to the flags, there were NRA stickers on the back bumper and the rear window. Hal immediately knew he had a "Florida Man", and followed him away from the prison.

A few miles down the road, the truck pulled into a bar and grill—what was referred to as a "honkytonk" in these parts of Florida—in the middle of nowhere, where citrus was grown, cattle were raised, and the houses were mostly trailers. There were a few other trucks parked in the lot, two towing airboats.

Hal watched as the prison guard climbed down from his truck and walked toward the "tonk", where he was intercepted by another man. Hal used his phone's camera to zoom in for a closer look and began recording what appeared to be a drug deal. Hal captured the entire transaction on video.

After the guard entered the bar, Hal waited for a few minutes before following him inside. Once seated at the bar, Hal ordered a Coke and glanced around, looking for the guard. He initially saw no sign of him, but soon the guard exited the bathroom and sat at the bar just a few seats away. When the guard ordered a beer, he appeared hyper and fidgety, fumbling with a few bills as he attempted to pay.

Hal had been around drug users enough in the past to know the guard was high on crystal. His pupils were dilated, and beads of sweat were visible on his forehead. Unable to sit still, the guard took his beer with him as he wandered around, stopping to chat with some guys playing pool.

When Hal finished his Coke, he strolled outside to his car and moved it alongside the guard's truck, backing in so the driver's sides were adjacent. There, Hal sat for an hour with the AC running while waiting for the guard to exit. When he did, Hal looked carefully for any sign of a firearm, but saw none. When the guard reached his truck, Hal rolled down his window and, with phone in hand, played the video to the guard. When the guard realized what he was watching, his face turned white.

"What would your boss say if he saw this?" Hal asked.

The guard said nothing, but his color turned from white to beet red, and he tried to snatch the phone away from Hal. Being quicker, Hal pulled in his phone and suddenly opened his door, slamming it hard into the guard, who fell to the ground. Hal exited his car and, with one swift kick, knocked the guard under the jacked-up truck with room to spare. With the flags still waving, and the guard peering out from under the truck like a weasel, Hal said, "You're going to do me a favor."

Holding his ribs in obvious pain, the guard asked, "What kind of favor?"

"I'm not sure yet. Come on out from under there, and we'll discuss it."

When the guard slid out from under his truck, Hal extended his hand to help him stand and said, "What's your name?"

Hal read the guard's face as he debated whether he should answer. When it appeared he'd decided no, taking a defiant posture, Hal placed his hand on the guard's neck and pressed his thumb on a spot that caused him to collapse on the ground once again.

"Give me your phone," Hal said. When the guard hesitated, Hal repeated, "Give me your phone, asshole!"

Defeated, the guard dug his phone out of his pocket and handed it to the man standing over him.

"What's your password?" Hal asked.

The guard again hesitated, and for the second time, Hal kicked him in the ribs, this time knocking the wind out of the guard. When he'd caught his breath, he said, "1996."

"Is that the year you were born? Very original," Hal mocked, before opening the phone and scrolling through the contacts, stopping at "Me." There, he found the guard's name, Walter Budd, along with an address, an email, and an emergency contact, Phyllis Budd.

"Walter, is Phyllis your wife or mother?

"My mother," he answered sheepishly.

Hal entered his own number into the phone and selected "Share Contact". When his phone buzzed, he replied to the text, "My new friend". Smirking, Hal said, "All right, Walter, I'll be in touch when it's time for you to do me the favor."

ATTORNEY JOHNNY ZIEGLER was waiting outside the judge's chambers for the lunch break to be over. When the hallway door opened, Johnny stood up to face Judge Halloran. "Good afternoon, Mr. Ziegler. Did you want to see me?"

"Yes, Your Honor, only for a minute."

"Sure, come in," the judge said, stepping back inside.

"Your Honor, we have reason to believe seven people are being held in Glades County Correction Center, who the prison will not acknowledge are there."

"And why are they there?"

"They were flown in from New York yesterday by ICE, who we believe plan to deport them without due process."

Judge Halloran let out a deep breath and shook his head. In a tone of disgust, he said, "What the fuck is going on with these cock-suckers? This secret deportation shit is becoming the norm!"

"My thoughts exactly, Your Honor."

"Do you have a Writ and a list of names?"

"I do, Sir," Johnny said, handing the judge a file.

"Good. You'll be second on this afternoon's docket. I'll look at your filing then."

"Thank you, Your Honor."

As Johnny walked down the hall toward the main courtroom entrance, a smile came over his face. Not just because he was about to get his case heard, but because of the salty language Judge Halloran used when outside the courtroom. After taking a seat in the second row, Johnny texted Seth to let him know he was about to present the Writ to the court.

When the first case concluded with a restraining order being granted against an abusive husband, it was time for Johnny to address the court. While Judge Halloran reviewed the file, Johnny made his way to the bench and stood patiently.

Repeating some of what he'd read for the courtroom stenographer, the judge said, "Mr. Ziegler, I see from your filing that you have reason to believe your clients are being held at the Glades County Jail without due process. Is that correct?"

"Yes, Your Honor."

"Have your clients had a court appearance or hearing of any kind anywhere in the United States?"

"Not to my knowledge, Your Honor."

"All right, this court will proceed with your Writ of Habeas Corpus, and will issue a subpoena for their appearance before this court at 10:00 a.m. tomorrow morning. That subpoena will go out immediately, but I can tell you from experience that the Glades County Jail may claim that its prisoners are unable to appear in this courtroom. If that is the case, the hearing will instead be held at the correctional facility at 10:00 a.m. tomorrow."

After the judge banged his gavel, Johnny said, "Thank you, Your Honor."

Once outside the courthouse, he called Seth.

"How'd you make out, Johnny?"

"All good. We have a hearing scheduled for tomorrow morning."

"Excellent! Would you like some co-counsel?"

"Sure. What do you know about Habeas Corpus?"

"I've been boning up on it all day. It might be good to bring Ariana Wilkinson's husband with me—he's a decorated Air Force Colonel, and makes a great impression in uniform."

"All right. Let me know when you're in town."

"Will do."

Knowing that Colonel Wilkinson was anxious for any report of progress, Seth called him. "I have some good news, Joe. We have a hearing scheduled in Glades County, Florida for tomorrow morning. I'll be there, and I'd like you to be there as well, if you can make it."

"Great! I've already made tentative plans for childcare. When are you thinking about going?"

"Tonight—I'll need to check for flights, though."

"I've already done that. JetBlue has non-stops out of White Plains into PBI at 5:20, 7:15, and 8:30."

Impressed that Joe already knew the available flights, Seth said, "Good. I doubt we'll make the 5:20, but the 7:15 is doable. Let's each make our own reservation and meet at the airport."

"Okay, see you there."

BY THE TIME Joe had his kids packed up, he hit the height of rush-hour traffic on his way to The Muslim Center and called Fatima to tell her they were on the way. As he said goodbye to his kids, Joe was pleased to see they were happy to be there with Fatima. Once at the airport, he made it through TSA just as the flight was boarding. Joe sidled alongside Seth in line, and they boarded together.

# CHAPTER 9

Mia had prepared a caprese salad for lunch, and somehow she'd found some good tomatoes—a near impossibility at this time of year. Afterward, she returned to her office while I cleaned up. With our plates in the dishwasher, I was wiping off the counter when Hal Baker called.

"Hey, Dan. I followed one of the prison guards when he left after his shift. To make a long story short, I witnessed him buying some crystal meth and captured it all on video."

"Where was this?"

"Outside a 'honkytonk' near the prison. He and I had a brief discussion in the parking lot, and let's just say he owes me a favor."

"Was the discussion friendly?" I asked, half joking.

"For the most part," Hal chuckled.

"Cool. That might be good to have in our back pocket."

"I thought so. I'm going to head back to West Palm if you have nothing more for me out here."

"Nope, thanks for the good work, Hal. I'll let you know if there's anything else."

As soon as I hung up, Seth called. "Things are coming to a head in Florida."

"Talk to me."

"Johnny Ziegler, my attorney friend, has a hearing scheduled for tomorrow morning."

"Does Joe know yet?"

"Yes, He's flying down with me tonight. I want him in the courtroom."

"I get it," I said. "Best of luck—let me know if there's anything I can do."

"Okay, Dan. I'll be in touch."

WITHOUT MUCH TO do until hearing from the guys in Florida, I thought about going down to my boat to finish preparing for the sailing season. Until I moved in with Mia, I lived aboard the boat while it was docked on City Island. She was a 43' Tartan, named *Privateer*, and she'd been hauled out of the water this past winter. After a fresh coat of bottom paint, we relaunched her a few weeks ago, and I'd been picking away at all the things needed to be done before leaving the dock. The last thing was installing the sails, which required two people.

I stuck my head in Mia's office door and asked, "When will you be finished with work for the day?"

She looked up at me and smiled. "I can knock off anytime."

"How about we go down to the boat for a few hours, and I'll take you to dinner at Sammy's?"

"Sure, that sounds wonderful. I can be ready in fifteen minutes."

"Great, sweetheart. I'll gather a few things."

**WHEN WE'D CLIMBED** aboard *Privateer* and opened the hatch, a familiar, pleasant scent emanated from below. Having been sealed up tight over the winter, boats often developed a stale, musty odor—sometimes worse. I had cleaned her thoroughly and hosed out the bilge, and today she smelled of fiberglass and varnish, exactly like she should. Mia and I spent half an hour installing the sails before I opened a bottle of chardonnay—we'd have our happy hour on the boat that afternoon.

While sitting in the cockpit watching the usual marina activity, Mia exclaimed, "What a delightful day! I'd forgotten how relaxing it is down here."

"It is nice, considering it's only the first week of May."

Over the afternoon, we chatted with a few of our dock mates, who'd also come out to enjoy the day. Eventually, as the sun dipped lower in the sky, the temperature began to drop, and having finished the wine, we wandered up to Sammy's.

City Island was primarily a row of seafood restaurants, some of which were a bit tacky, interspersed with boatyards and marine supply stores. We liked Sammy's the best, not just for the food, but for the bar crowd, who were mostly sailors. It was also the closest place to our marina.

As we often did, we ordered the crab platter, which was more than enough for the two of us. It came with King crab, Dungeness crab, and crab cakes, along with French fries and coleslaw.

While our dinner was being prepared, Mia asked, "What's the latest on your immigrant case?"

"They're in a prison in Florida awaiting deportation. I've had another PI working on it, and Seth hired an attorney down there. There's a court hearing scheduled for tomorrow morning."

"Will that be the end of it?"

"If you asked me a few months ago, I would have said yes. Hell, this wouldn't have even happened a few months ago. However, I now have no idea—Florida seems to have its own interpretation of the law."

"Isn't this federal law?"

"Exactly," I replied skeptically, raising my eyebrows

**THE NEXT MORNING,** I heard from Seth. "Hey Dan, I wanted to let you know the hearing will be held at the prison."

"Why's that?"

"The federal prosecutor claims they can't all be transported to the courthouse. Attorney Ziegler says it's a common tactic they use, simply to be uncooperative and hope for a delay. But Judge Halloran was prepared for this and will hear the case there."

"Okay, is there anything I can do?"

"Yeah, give me the contact info for the PI you hired down here. Just in case we need some legwork."

"Sure, I'll text it right over. And I'll give him a heads up that you might be calling."

"Great, Dan. Thanks."

After texting each of them, I had a sense I'd be called on again that day. There was no real reason—just an intuition I'd developed over the years.

# CHAPTER 10

When Seth and Joe checked into the Airport Hotel in West Palm, Joe insisted on paying the bill. "Look, I know you took this case pro bono. The least I can do is pick up the tab for the hotel."

"All right, but if there are two beds, we can share the room, if that's okay with you."

"Hey, you're talking to a guy who's shared barracks with dozens of guys for years. It's not a problem for me."

"Okay, one room it is."

After grabbing a tall Scotch and a bite to eat at the hotel bar, they went up to the room and were asleep within minutes.


SETH WENT DOWN for breakfast while Joe was still getting dressed. When Joe joined him, Seth said, "You make quite an impression with all the medals, Colonel."

"This is what twenty years gets you." Joe smiled modestly.

While Joe was at the buffet, Seth got a call from Johnny Ziegler.

"Good morning, Seth."

"Good morning, Johnny. Are we all set for the hearing?"

"Yes. It'll take you about an hour and twenty minutes with traffic. Do you need directions?"

"I'll just use a phone app. Glades County Correctional in Moore Haven?"

"That's it."

"I have Colonel Wilkinson with me. We'll be there before ten."

"All right, I'll see you then."

When Joe returned with a full plate, Seth told him about the drive.

"Is it usual for a hearing to be held at a jail?" Joe asked.

"It's not *unusual*. I'm sure the DOJ is making this as difficult as possible. Luckily, the judge is willing to play their game."

"Okay, as long as I can see my wife."

"I'm sure she's looking forward to seeing you, too. If things go well, we'll be taking her home with us, but I must warn you that the federal prosecutor will do everything in his power to prevent that."

Joe's face sank, along with his shoulders. "How can they do that?"

"Look, I'm hopeful they won't, but this new regime in Washington is micro-managing everything. It will just be a delaying tactic if they do. *We* are on the right side of the law."

Joe just sat there, pushing his food around his plate. When it was time to pick up the rental car, he'd only managed to eat half of his breakfast.

While in the car, Seth called Dan to bring him up to date on the hearing. They managed to arrive at the jail with just minutes to spare.

"COLONEL WILKINSON. I presume?" Johnny Ziegler greeted as they entered the prison.

"Yes, Sir. Call me Joe."

Seth finished the introductions, and everyone shook hands. They then sat in an interview room, located just off the entrance. Seth noticed that Joe took off his hat whenever he was inside, holding it formally against his chest, unless he was seated, in which case he'd set it down.

Johnny glanced at Seth and smiled. "You haven't aged a bit since law school, Seth."

"Yeah, thanks, *ha ha*," Seth replied sarcastically, knowing how unusually youthful he appeared. "Are you considering me co-counsel today?"

"I think so, they're your clients after all."

"That's fine, I just wanted to know how you intend to play it with this judge."

"Yeah, I've told him about you. He's on our side."

"That's good to know. I'd prefer if you lead, though."

Johnny nodded, and Seth said, "Joe, do you have any questions for Johnny?"

After clearing his throat, Joe asked, "What would you like from me today?"

"Just sit in the court quietly, while everyone admires your uniform and all-American appearance. If you are asked a question, answer it honestly and confidently—no worries."

"All right," Joe sighed, his shoulders relaxing.

A moment later, the doors opened, and the three of them entered the makeshift courtroom. Johnny led them to a table in the front, across the aisle from the government team, who introduced themselves like they were all old buddies.

They hadn't been seated a minute when a side door opened, and the seven detainees from New York were led inside. All were handcuffed and shackled except for the girl. When Joe saw Ariana restrained that way, he gritted his teeth to keep his composure. Once they were seated, Ariana snuck a peek at him, making eye contact with a smile only he could read: *I'm so happy to see you!*

A moment later, the judge entered the makeshift courtroom and took a seat facing everyone.

Judge Halloran announced, "Since we're in this room today, we'll keep this hearing casual. I have a list of attendees today, and I recognize some of you. I assume you have introduced yourselves to one another?" He nodded at the front tables.

"Yes, Your Honor," Cameron Henry, the prosecutor, replied.

"Good, shall we get right to it then?" Again, he looked to those in front. Seeing nods in the affirmative, Judge Halloran continued, "I've reviewed the case files and see that all of the detainees are in this country legally by one means or another. Mr. Henry, why are they here today?"

"Your Honor, the Department of Homeland Security has charged us with detaining every immigrant from a Muslim country regardless of their status."

"It's the 'regardless of their status' part of your statement that troubles me, Mr. Henry. Are you familiar with the Constitution of the United States?"

"Of course, Your Honor." He feigned being insulted by the question.

A woman from the government table rose and said, "If I may, Your Honor, I'm Leslie Nixon from the Attorney General's Office. I can assure you that we have many attorneys in the AG's department with the legal opinion that Immigration and Customs Enforcement has the right to deport anyone upon instruction from the President."

"Ms. Nixon, I disagree with that opinion, and it's my opinion that counts here today. This is how I would like to proceed: Mr. Ziegler, may the court hear from the detainees personally?"

The prosecutor stood. "I object, Your Honor. If the court would like statements from the prisoners, I demand that they be under oath and that we have the opportunity to cross-examine them."

"Relax, Mr. Henry. I said we would do this in a casual manner today. Mr. Ziegler?"

"I have no objection, Your Honor."

"All right, would the first person on my left state your name and tell me how you arrived in this country?" The judge nodded to the man on the far end.

Appearing extremely nervous, the man nodded to said, "My name is Muhammad Bashire. Eleven years ago, my brother came to this country from Pakistan to start a painting business. When he saved up enough money, he sent for my brother and me with tickets to join him in America. Since then, we have grown the business to one of the largest in the city of Yonkers. I got my Green Card in 2018, and I follow every law."

"Thank you, Muhammad. Nothing in your file indicates otherwise." The judge nodded to the next person. "Ma'am?"

"Yes, sir. I am Farah Noor, and this is my daughter, Mariam, who is an American citizen. Her father and I came here from Iraq to escape the war. We were granted asylum in 2010, and Mariam was born in New York in 2019."

Each of them told their story, the judge reviewing their files as they spoke. The last to speak was Ariana.

"Good morning, Your Honor. My name is Ariana Wilkinson. I came here from Afghanistan, where I was an interpreter and advisor to the United States Armed Forces. It was during the war that I married Colonel Joseph Wilkinson, who is here in this room today."

All eyes went to Joe, the only one in uniform.

Ariana continued, "He brought me to America at the end of the war as his wife. I know we followed all the rules. I am a legal resident and have an appointment next month to become a citizen. We also have two children born in the United States—Katie, who is three, and Joe Jr., who is one and a half. I miss them terribly, Your Honor."

When she finished, she turned to Joe and smiled. He smiled back proudly and heard a groan from the government table.

"Thank you all," Judge Halloran said. "Does anyone else have something to say to the court?"

Everyone at the government table leaped to their feet, Cameron Henry leading the way. "Your Honor, we object! May we question the prisoners?"

"Again, Mr. Henry, we are trying to keep this casual. Do you have any evidence that what each of them told us here today is untrue?"

The government team huddled, whispering with one another, until Cameron said, "Your Honor, we were not aware we'd have the opportunity to present evidence today. We're unprepared at this time."

"I'll note for the record that you were unprepared. I, however, am prepared to make a ruling. This court finds for the petitioners, each and every one of them. I hereby order their immediate release. In addition, I order the Justice Department to compensate them for any expenses incurred while returning to their homes."

Cameron Henry again leaped to his feet. "Your Honor, we will appeal this decision. I urge you to delay your verdict pending that appeal."

"My verdict stands, Mr. Henry. You have until 3:00 this afternoon to present a stay from the superior court. Otherwise, they're to be released. This hearing is adjourned."

We all stood as the judge left the room. What had been joy on the faces of the detainees just a moment ago had now given way to bewilderment, as they wondered what it all meant. The government team hurried out of the room, while Seth and Johnny explained the verdict to the detainees.

With just a few guards at the doors, Joe and Ariana rushed to each other and embraced, hugging for all they were worth.

"Don't worry, honey, you'll be home soon," Joe said. "I won't leave here without you."

As the guards led their captives back to their cell, Seth, Joe, and Johnny returned to the interview room. "What just happened?" Joe asked.

"The good news is the judge ruled in our favor. The bad news is that the government has the right to appeal, and the appellate court may stay this decision pending the outcome of their hearing. In practical terms, that means they may be held prisoner until that court rules."

"And how long will that take?"

Johnny answered, "It will be a matter of days, not weeks. But let's not get ahead of ourselves. There's a good chance they'll be free by 3:00."

None of what Joe heard made him feel better. He felt like he was being kicked around by the government he'd sworn an oath to, twenty years ago. The more he thought about it, the angrier he became, working his jaw.

To change the mood, Johnny said, "Since we'll be waiting around until 3:00, we might as well go out to lunch. Although, sadly, the best restaurant around here is a Popeye's."

"Let's go, gentlemen, it's on me," Joe announced, hoping that getting out of there would relieve his anger.

AFTER EATING, WITH nowhere else to go, they lingered at the restaurant drinking coffee while Seth and Johnny reminisced about their days in law school. To Joe, it sounded remarkably similar to his time in college. As he began to recall those days, his mind leaped back to the image of Ariana in handcuffs and shackles, his anger returning

A few minutes after 2:00, Johnny got a call from Judge Halloran: "I'm sorry, Johnny, but the appeals court issued the stay."

"Shit. I was afraid they would, given the politics of this state."

"Yeah, I suspected they would, too. That doesn't mean we can't have a bond hearing, though—your clients certainly don't pose a danger to society. If they waive their rights to appear, I'll schedule that for tomorrow morning at the courthouse with just the lawyers.

"Thank you for that, judge. I'll obtain the waivers and be prepared to argue the case."

"Don't work too hard on it, Johnny. I'm inclined just to release them on their own recognizance."

"Thank you, judge. Would you suppose Colonel Wilkinson can visit his wife this afternoon?"

"Yes. I'll call over there and make sure of it."

"Great, we'll see you in the morning."

Joe and Seth had overheard enough of the conversation to be disappointed, their faces glum.

"Let's go visit your wife, Colonel," said Johnny.

While on their way back to the prison, Johnny filled them in on the bond hearing and the judge's intent. When the three of them entered together and asked to see Ariana, the guard was ready for them and said, "Have a seat in the interview room, gentlemen. I'll have Ms. Wilkinson brought to you."

A few minutes later, Ariana entered without restraints of any kind.

Seth said, "We'll leave you two alone. Take all the time you need."

When it was just Joe and Ariana in the room, they hugged and kissed, standing with their bodies pressed together, and tears in their eyes. Joe said, "The kids are fine. Fatima is taking care of them until we get back, which hopefully will be tomorrow." Ariana looked at Joe with a questioning expression, and he explained Judge Halloran's intent to release them on bond.

Rubbing her wrists, she said, "I'll believe it when it happens, Joe. I've gotten my hopes up, only to be disappointed too many times in the last few days."

"I understand, honey. But I'm here now, and as I said, I'm not leaving without you."

They were allowed to spend an hour together, alone in the room, where they mostly discussed the kids and Joe's renewed discovery of their abilities and personalities. They ended up having some happy moments, with brief episodes of laughter. But mainly, they touched and held each other, lifting Ariana's spirits.

Seth, Joe, and Johnny began the drive back to West Palm, mainly in silence. It'd been an emotional day, and there wasn't much left to say. About halfway there, Joe's phone rang. It was Major Willis.

"What's up, J.T.?"

"Hey, Joe. I'm still watching for flight plans, and just saw one come across for an ICE flight. It's leaving Joint Base Andrews sometime after midnight, going to Sebring. I thought you might like to know about it."

Realizing the gravity of this new information, Joe focused instantly. "What type of plane is it?"

"An Embraer 145. A regional jet that holds up to fifty passengers."

"Fuck! It sounds like they're going to move them again before being released tomorrow." Seth and Johnny's ears perked up at Joe's last statement. "Can I call you right back, J.T.?"

"I'll be standing by."

When Joe had filled them in on the whole conversation, Seth asked, "Should we notify Judge Halloran, Johnny?"

"I don't know. Those bastards seem hell bent on defying the laws. I'm not sure there's much the judge can do."

"Maybe we need to handle this ourselves," Joe suggested.

"How do you mean?" Seth asked.

"I mean, physically prevent them from boarding the plane."

"You mean with force, like a military action?"

"Perhaps. I haven't thought it through yet, but I'm open to ideas."

"Let me call Dan."

"Good idea," Joe agreed.

"Who's Dan?" Johnny asked.

"My investigator," Seth replied. "He's rescued people before without running afoul of the law."

Without waiting for a response from Johnny, Seth punched in Dan's number on speed dial.

"Hey, Seth. How are you making out in Florida?"

"That's why I'm calling. While the judge ruled in our favor, the detainees are still being held pending appeal, and we just found out that ICE intends to fly them out overnight."

"Out of the country?"

"Probably. The only thing we know is there's an inbound flight arriving in Sebring in the early morning hours. I'm hoping you have some ideas."

"Let me call Hal, my PI friend in West Palm—he knows the lay of the land. I'll get back to you in a few minutes."

"Okay, thanks, Dan."

While waiting for Dan to call back, Joe called J.T. "Any updates?"

"Nothing on the flight plan, but a thought just ran through my mind: What if you and I commandeer the aircraft and fly them out of there?"

"That's pretty bold, J.T. We'd be hijacking a United States government airplane. Even if we pulled it off, we'd be chased by F-35s and forced to land. I mean, it's not like we're still in the Middle East."

"Maybe there's a way to do it without them knowing it."

"Maybe, but for the moment, we should try to do this legally."

"All right, Joe. Just keep it in mind—I'm willing to help."

"Thanks. Let me know if there are any changes to the flight plan."

"Will do."

While Joe was wrapping up his call, Seth got a call back from Dan. "I'm on my way down there. We need to put our heads together and devise a plan. If our clients are removed from the country, they may never be seen again."

"What time do you get in?"

"7:00 at PBI. Hal will pick me up—where should we meet?"

After conferring with Johnny briefly, Seth replied, "At a law office in West Palm. I'll forward the info."

It was 5:00 by the time Seth, Joe, and Johnny arrived at the office. They had remained quiet, deep in thought, as they drove. Once there, Johnny put on a pot of coffee, and they sat in the conference room to devise a plan.

"What legal remedies do we have?" Seth asked.

Johnny thought for a few moments and said, "Maybe Judge Halloran can order the warden to keep the detainees there until tomorrow's hearing."

"Would the warden follow that order?"

"I don't know. The Governor is the warden's direct superior. He would probably do whatever the Governor tells him to do."

Joe, still in uniform, spoke next: "Can we contact the Governor?"

Johnny chucked and replied, "You've been out of the country too long, Joe. Governor DeSantis is the most MAGA Governor in the country. There's no way he'll take our side on this. Hell, he'd deport them himself if he knew they were Muslims."

Seth nodded, agreeing with his fellow attorney. "Let's come up with a few plans of action before Dan and Hal get here. Then we'll get their input and see where we go from there."

Over the next two hours, they filled legal pads with ideas, bouncing them off one another. When the coffee pot was drained, Johnny put on a fresh one and ordered some pizzas to be delivered. By 7:30, Dan and Hal arrived.

After everyone was introduced, they reviewed the possibilities that they'd come up with so far. There were a few ideas based on preventing them from getting on the plane, preventing the plane from landing or from taking off. The last two involved blocking the runway. Another was putting together a crew to impersonate ICE agents, going to the prison, then driving off with the detainees before the real ICE agents arrived. For that to work, they'd need to make sure the real agents weren't in communication with the prison, perhaps by disabling the phone lines. But with the widespread use of cell phones, that idea went to the bottom of the list.

Joe told them about Major Willis's plan to hijack the plane once the detainees were on board. While Joe was certainly capable of flying the plane, what would they do with the original pilots?

With none of the plans leading to a eureka moment, Dan said, "Hal, tell them about the compromised guard."

"Okay, when I was out there poking around a few days ago, I witnessed a drug deal going down, involving one of the prison guards at a 'honkytonk' on the outskirts of town. I recorded the whole thing on my phone and showed it to him. Needless to say, he doesn't want me to show the video to the warden, so I told him he'd need to do me a favor at a time of my choosing. I'm pretty sure he'll comply when asked. He's also physically afraid of me."

Johnny said, "Maybe we can use him to leave a door open, or to create a distraction at an opportune time."

"Maybe. I'll text him to see when he's on duty."

"You can text him?" Johnny asked, surprised.

"Yeah, we shared contacts with each other. As I told you, he's afraid of me."

Seth laughed, "He must be!"

A few moments later, Hal said, "He's on duty from midnight to 8:00 a.m."

"Perfect," Seth said.

Dan then asked, "What are your thoughts, Joe?"

"Whichever way we do this, I don't want to *just* get them out of prison; I want to get them out of this entire fucking state. We need to get them back to New York—or at least to someplace with a functioning legal system."

"I agree," Seth said.

Hal asked, "If we're thinking of hijacking a plane, wouldn't it be easier to hijack the bus instead?"

"And take them where?" Johnny wondered.

"Maybe to another airport—we could charter a plane," Seth suggested.

"All right, we've got too many balls in the air here," Dan said. "Hal, can you contact the guard and find out what he might be able to do for us?"

"On it," he replied while texting.

"Let me check for an update on the flight plan," Joe said.

As the two of them worked their phones, Dan spoke softly with the lawyers. "We're talking about a lot of illegal shit here. Are you guys really willing to put your careers on the line?"

Seth replied, "I think I can speak for both of us; We aren't going to personally take part in the hijacking of an airplane or a bus, or breaking anyone out of jail. We're acting as legal advisors, protected by the attorney-client privilege. Considering that, we may be the least liable people in this room."

Johnny nodded.

Dan paused, considering what Seth had just explained, then said, "Okay, let's review the possibilities. Is it even doable to put together a group, dress up as ICE agents, and take them out of the prison before the real agents show up?"

Seth and Johnny shook their heads.

"Okay, let's scratch that from the list. Is there anything we can ask Judge Halloran to do for us?"

"Nothing he hasn't previously done. He's already ordered them to be held until the hearing tomorrow," Johnny replied.

"All right, so there is no legal action we can take, correct?"

The lawyers shook their heads.

"The list is getting shorter," Dan stated.

While that conversation was taking place, Joe was speaking with Major Willis: "There's no change to the flight plan, Joe. No new plans have been filed by ICE going into Florida, at least not as yet."

"Good to know."

"Look, I'm still willing to come out there and help you with the plane, but I'll need to get moving now if you want a copilot."

"I appreciate the offer, J.T., but I can't let you jeopardize your whole career and your retirement—you're too close. We'll find another way."

"All right, buddy. Good luck."

HAL LOOKED UP from his phone after pecking away on it for the last few minutes. "The guard, whose name is Walter, says that on an overnight shift, they're lightly staffed, maybe three or four of them in total, unless prisoners are coming and going. If that's the case, there may be a couple more, and he's likely to be the one to escort them in or out. He said the best he can do is keep me notified of the movement. He can't leave a door unlocked because they automatically close and lock, although he might be able to open a door for us."

"At the hearing, I noticed the guards' uniforms consisted of just a shirt and a baseball cap. They were all wearing blue jeans and a variety of shoe styles," Johnny said.

"That's what he was wearing when I saw him at the tonk," Hal added.

"Ask him if he has a spare uniform he can give us," Johnny said.

Hal sent another text, then read the reply: "Yes."

"Good. If we want it, we'll just have to arrange to get it from him."

"What are you thinking, Johnny?" Dan asked.

"I'm thinking one of you might be able to pass as a guard by wearing one of his shirts and hats."

"Dan, you're the only one thin enough to fit into one of his shirts. And they're short sleeves, so your long arms won't matter," Hal observed.

"So, what are we thinking?" Dan asked.

"Sounds like we're either hijacking the bus or the plane," Joe concluded.

# CHAPTER 11

The plan started to come together a few minutes after midnight. J.T. notified Joe that the ICE flight had taken off. Walter informed Hal that he'd been assigned to accompany some prisoners on a bus to the airport, and that he'd be armed with a shotgun and a sidearm. Walter also confirmed that he'd left a uniform shirt and hat in the bed of his truck.

The plan was for Dan, while wearing the guard's shirt, to join Walter on the bus to the airport, and Hal and Joe would follow the bus in Hal's minivan. Then Dan and Walter would force the driver to stop the bus along the way, where they'd transfer the passengers to the minivan and drive away. They had also assumed that Walter would be the only one armed. There were a lot of moving parts and assumptions in the plan, and they knew they'd likely have to improvise on the fly. What they were most unsure of was how much they could rely on Walter.

"What if your guard informs the warden of our plan? They could be lying in wait for us," Dan cautioned.

"I doubt he'd do that. He knows that I know where his mother lives."

The two attorneys looked at each other for a moment, then shrugged.

Seth said, "Okay, we're on."

By knowing when the flight took off, Joe could estimate its arrival time at Sebring between 2:30 and 2:45 a.m. If the intent was to have the passengers there when the plane arrived, the bus might leave the prison as early as 1:30. They needed to get on the road right away.

Joe and Dan rode with Hal, while Seth rode with Johnny. Fortunately, traffic was light, and they pulled onto the prison lot with a few minutes to spare.

Hal and Walter had been in touch along the way, and Walter suggested that Dan follow the bus through the gate on foot. To retrieve the clothing from Walter's jacked up truck, Hal had to give Dan a boost up to the back bumper so he could reach over the tailgate to access the bed.

After Dan put on the shirt and hat, it was another twenty minutes before the bus arrived. As the gate opened, Hal identified Walter as the one who opened it, and Dan casually wandered in behind the bus before the gate closed behind him.

With a nod of their heads, Dan and Walter acknowledged each other silently as Walter introduced Dan to the driver as the new guy. Walter then went in to retrieve the prisoners, while Dan remained on the bus. He spoke as little as possible to the driver, yawning and acting tired and disinterested.

ARIANA HAD BEEN tossing and turning while the others were sleeping. The hallway lights had been dimmed quite a while ago, and while her body clock told her it was the wee hours of the morning, she sensed something was up. What that was, she didn't know. She could have heard a pin drop.

When the lights came back on, including the lights in their cell, she sat up, wondering what was going on. She wouldn't let herself think of being released; it would be too painful if they weren't. Two guards entered the cell, pulling a cart loaded with shackles, and began putting them on the detainees, two at a time, while another guard stood by the door observing. Once they had all been shackled and were led outside to a waiting bus, Ariana felt for sure they were about to be deported. *The only question was where—what awful country would they be taken to?* She began to cry. Seth and her husband had told her there would be a hearing today, and she would be released.

Twenty minutes later, Walter led the detainees onto the bus with the shotgun by his side. They managed to take a seat without much trouble, despite the restraints. After the driver started the engine and approached the gate, he stopped to open the door. Another guard stepped aboard, armed just like Walter, and walked all the way to the back without saying a word.

*Shit*, Dan thought. *There goes the plan to take the detainees off the bus.*

Once they were on the road, riding in the dark, moonless night, Dan texted Joe to inform him of the late addition of a second armed guard. It took a while for a reply, and Dan hoped they were devising an alternate plan, but when the reply came, their text simply read, "We go with Plan B."

**WHILE EN ROUTE** to the airport, Joe downloaded the important numbers pertaining to this aircraft, along with a couple of checklists.

While it wasn't flying instructions, there were numbers a pilot needed to know, such as stall speed, approach speed under various configurations, maximum rate of climb speed, and so on. It was certainly a less complicated aircraft than the fighter jets he'd flown.

HAL KEPT HIS minivan a comfortable distance behind the bus to remain unnoticed as they approached the airport. When the prison bus reached the dark, desolate airport, they found an open gate in the chain link fence, allowing them to drive onto the tarmac. With the headlights off, Hal stopped a hundred feet short of the fence, where Joe hopped out and followed the bus through the gate on foot, unseen by anyone. It was immediately obvious which plane they were looking for, even without any markings: it was the only jet large enough to accommodate the group, and it was well lit with the door open and folding stairs deployed. Dan took a deep breath to calm his nerves—the next few minutes were where the whole plan could come apart.

Joe, in uniform, wearing his hat decorated to identify his senior rank, was the first to board the airplane, followed closely behind by Dan in the guard's uniform. Walter and the other guard remained on the bus with the prisoners.

Joe went directly to the cockpit where he announced, "Gentlemen, you have the rest of the night off." As the pilots looked at each other, confused, Joe continued, "This plane will be going to a location known only to the President and the Secretary of Homeland Security. Another plane will arrive shortly to take you home."

Unwilling to question the authority of an Air Force Colonel, the pilots again looked at each other, then shrugged and climbed out of their seats. Once they'd exited the aircraft, Dan motioned to

Walter to begin boarding the prisoners. As they were being seated, Dan's heart rate continued to climb as he became impatient with how long it was taking.

When they were finally seated, Dan instructed Walter to remove their restraints, while Joe started the engines and familiarized himself with the aircraft. As soon as Walter exited the plane, Dan threw a lever that raised the stairs and closed the door, then joined Joe in the cockpit. He watched as Joe went through the pre-flight checklist, checking fuel levels, adjusting the flap settings, and flipping a myriad of switches.

While Joe was doing all this, Dan's heart raced as he looked out the windshield, expecting someone to stop them at any moment. When Joe finally began taxiing toward the runway, Dan thought, *We just might pull this off!*

Once on the runway, Joe lined them up on the centerline and shoved the throttles forward, the thrust pinning them back in their seats. They were airborne moments later, and after raising the landing gear, the two of them bumped fists.

After takeoff, Joe remembered to turn off the transponder, an electronic device that would identify the aircraft on air traffic control radar screens. A few minutes later, they leveled off at seventeen thousand feet, as Joe explained to Dan, "Anything higher than this requires a flight plan, and we don't want anyone to know we're even in the air, although we won't be able to reach maximum cruising speed at this altitude."

As they headed north in the night sky, a call came in over the radio from air traffic control asking if they'd taken off yet. Apparently, the pilots had filed a flight plan with an estimated take-off time that'd already passed. Joe told ATC they had experienced mechanical issues and canceled the flight plan. With the transponder off, they may still appear as a small blip on a radar screen, but would likely remain unnoticed.

"Where are we going, Colonel?" Dan asked.

"I thought we would land in Montgomery, New York. There's an airport up there that was built fifty years ago with a really long runway. Plus, it's in the middle of nowhere, and there won't be anyone in the tower at this time of night."

"Sounds like you've thought this through. We'll need someone to pick us up, though."

"Seth already arranged that while you were on the bus."

Dan just nodded, impressed with the plan.

"I'm going to go back and speak with Ariana. Don't worry, the autopilot is flying the plane."

"Is there anything you want me to do?"

"Yeah, don't touch anything," Joe quipped.

**DESPITE THE DIM** lighting in the passenger cabin, when Ariana saw Joe exit the cockpit, her eyes opened wide with shock. Joe sat next to her and took her in his arms.

"Oh my god, Joe. I thought we were going to El Salvador! Or someplace equally terrible. I feared I'd never see you again!" She began to cry.

"I told you I wouldn't leave without you, honey. Everything will be all right," he said as she clung to him, coming to grips with her good fortune.

When she did, she announced to the other passengers that the pilot was her husband, and they were going home. The others looked around in disbelief.

Joe remained seated with Ariana for a few more minutes, until he felt she was comfortable with everything that was happening. After a kiss, he returned to the cockpit and checked their progress on the GPS. They were approaching North Carolina, and Joe wanted to steer well clear of the DC area, where air traffic control would be most vigilant. He turned the plane ten degrees to the east, so they'd be out over the Atlantic when passing the nation's capital.

Dan said, "You know, we're all likely to be arrested as soon as they find out what we've done. Are you concerned about the consequences of all this?"

"I haven't given it a thought. Do you have a family, Dan?"

"I have a twenty-one-year-old daughter named Hannah."

"Then you understand how you'd risk everything to protect her."

Dan's shoulders shivered. "I certainly do. This time last year, some crooked cops kidnapped Hannah and held her in a cabin in Connecticut. Three friends and I rescued her in a military-style raid with flash-bangs and the whole nine yards. We ended up killing two of the cops."

Joe studied Dan's face for a moment and saw something he'd only seen from soldiers in combat. He nodded and refocused on flying the airplane.

THE SKY WAS clear when they passed over Long Island with the lights of the New York skyline shining brightly to the west. They heard some joyful sounds from the passenger cabin, and Dan said, "Welcome home, Colonel!"

It was still dark when they landed, and after taxiing off the runway at the deserted airport, there was only one vehicle inside the gate. It was an extended full-size van driven by Dan's closest friends, Jim Abbott and Matt Frost, two of the guys who helped rescue Hannah.

With everyone loaded in the van, Jim headed south along the Hudson River. Dan's first call was to Seth, who was sitting at PBI, waiting for the first flight out. After a few questions about how it unfolded on the plane, Seth asked Dan to put him on speaker so he could advise everyone on how to handle what they were about to face.

Seth began, "Don't say anything to anyone about where you are, or where you were, except for your closest loved ones, or an attorney if you have one. If you do have an attorney, call them. I'll be contacting the media and civil rights groups to create support for your cause and to organize protests. The most important and urgent thing I can do is get public opinion on your side before the government begins its campaign to demonize you. They will do that, so be prepared.

"ICE may come after you again, but before they do, I'll make sure everyone knows your story and what you've been through. They'll also know that you are all documented and here legally. My goal is to make it as difficult as possible for them to detain you again.

"You may want to gather at your mosque to support each other, and ICE has been hesitant to conduct raids at a place of worship. I believe you all have my contact information, so please don't hesitate to call my office with any questions or to report an incident.

Paula, my paralegal, will be able to assist you with anything you need and she'll serve as our clearinghouse for information. Best of luck to you all."

Everyone on the bus clapped and cheered for Seth's efforts. As they continued toward New York, they all called their loved ones to let them know they were safe and arranged for a ride home. It took over an hour to reach the Mosque in Mt. Vernon, where most of the people were dropped off. Jim drove the others home, including Joe, Ariana, and Dan.

The sun had risen by the time Joe and Ariana entered their home. They immediately showered, Ariana scrubbing the essence of prison from her body. Once clean, their time in the shower became more intimate, as they rediscovered each other after being apart for a year. Soon they were in bed, making love tenderly, until falling asleep in the comfort of each other's arms.

# CHAPTER 12

'd called Mia on the way back from the airport, well before sunrise. I kept her informed during my time in Florida, and she was aware of our plans to free the detainees. However, she had no idea that we'd hijacked a plane.

She greeted me at the door in her signature silk loungewear, and gave me a serious kiss when I was inside. Her outfit was like dressy pajamas—loose and comfortable, but the way it draped over her form was incredibly sexy. After leading me to the kitchen, she poured me coffee while preparing a big breakfast. Sipping and watching her cook reminded me how hungry I was—and how much I'd missed her. She served scrambled eggs with bacon and sausage, along with toast and home fries, which was something she rarely made. Our usual breakfast was much healthier, with fewer calories—typically fruit and yogurt.

While eating, I replayed my last twelve hours, blow by blow. Her mouth dropped open when I told her about commandeering an airplane and flying it to New York. Then a look of concern came over her face, and she said, "Dan, you're scaring me. Am I going to have to worry about you every time you leave the house?"

"I hope you don't, but there was no other way. I always thought I was working *for* the government, not against it."

"Dan, you're retired!"

"Semi-retired," I corrected, setting my fork down.

"If you're putting your life in danger, that's not semi-retired." Mia's reaction caught me off guard, and I knew I was walking on thin ice.

"Sweetheart, being a cop is different than a regular job. It just is."

"Then stop being a cop—you're *not* one anymore. A private investigator does not need to put their life on the line."

"You're making it out to be more dangerous than it is. Half the time, Jim and I are sitting in the office, tracing the ownership of cars."

"I know, Dan. But since I met you, you've been in a gunfight on the streets of Brooklyn, organized and led a military-style raid, leaving two people dead. You had a wild chase on the open ocean in a small boat while being shot at, and now you hijacked a government plane? And that's all in the period of a little more than a year! Do you still think I'm making it sound more dangerous than it is?"

I had no comeback for that. It was true, every word of it. This was the closest we'd ever come to an argument, and it rocked me. Sometimes the truth hurts, and my head sagged as I remembered that this was exactly what came between me and Sheila, my first wife: her fear of my leaving the house and not coming back.

Mia sensed my anguish, slid her chair closer, and put her hand on the back of my neck, easing the tension. She could have said *You don't need to work; I have plenty of money for both of us.* But Mia knew better—she was aware of my sensitivity to that situation.

We remained quiet for a while, until she said, "Look, I shouldn't have unloaded on you like that—it just all came out at once. But you scare the bejesus out of me sometimes, Dan. I can't lose you. You've filled a void in my life, a void I didn't even know existed before I met you."

I finally picked my head up and looked at her, meeting her eyes, sharing emotions at a base level deeper than any words could convey.

"I guess I'll need to reconsider my work. You've made that clear."

Mia put her arms around me with her head buried in my chest, happy that I understood. We held each other for a while, until she said, "You must be exhausted."

"I am. I just want to shower and climb into bed."

"Just?"

I finally smiled. "Well, maybe not *just*."

"Finish your breakfast and go ahead up. I'll join you in a minute," she said, before offering me a taste of her lips.

I ENDED UP sleeping until mid-afternoon, and when I came downstairs. Mia was in her office working. "Good afternoon, love. Feeling rested?"

"Much better, thanks."

"You might want to turn on the news; it seems you're the lead story. Again!"

Mia was right; all the cable networks were running loops of the empty plane on the tarmac, just as we left it, with the door open and the stairs resting on the ground. CNN and MSNBC were showing clips of Seth and Imam Khan praising us as heroes. Over on Fox, a spokesperson from the Department of Homeland Security made it sound like we'd committed treason. But by the time the major networks' evening news came on, they were showing taped interviews of some of the Muslims that we'd delivered home to their families.

It was clear that Seth had successfully laid the groundwork with the media, and more importantly, the public. There were man-on-the-street interviews with people expressing their outrage at the government for trying to deport good people who were here lawfully. While there was a different spin on Fox News, Seth had won the first day.

I made us cocktails, a bit later than usual, and sat in the kitchen while Mia cooked dinner. After another wonderful meal, I called Matt Frost, my former NYPD partner. "Hey, Frosty. I wanted to thank you for going out in the middle of the night to pick us up."

"No worries, Dan. I was happy to help when Jim called. I assume you've been watching the news?"

"I have."

"My old partner, a national hero once again. How do you manage to get yourself involved in these things?"

"I'm just lucky, I guess. Or maybe unlucky, if the authorities come after me."

"I'm sure they will, Dan. This president can't stand it when someone shows him up."

"You're right. I've already seen his Heinrich Himmler wanna-be deputy chief of staff on TV. Seth has his work cut out for him."

"I'll say. Let's get together for a beer while you're still a free man," Frosty quipped, laughing.

"You got it, pal."

After the call ended, I feared that Frosty had a point. A sobering point.

**THE FOLLOWING DAY,** while sipping coffee with Mia, we again saw Seth on TV. He was holding a press conference in front of a courthouse in Manhattan, surrounded by protesters chanting and holding signs that read: "Humans Aren't Illegal" and "Save Religious Freedom." Other signs expressed similar sentiment, including one that read, "Where's the Due Process?" I assumed Seth had rallied the support among some human rights activists that he knew.

When he stepped to the microphone, the crowd hushed. "Ladies and gentlemen, thank you for coming out today in support of these hard-working, *legal* residents. In one hour, all of them, except for the minor child, will surrender themselves in this courthouse before Judge Kennedy. He will make them available to Immigration and Customs Enforcement for interviews. If they're charged with a crime, he will hear their cases immediately. Since they are all here lawfully, I can only assume he will rule in their favor and allow them to stay in this country if they so choose. I have time for a few questions."

The crowd of reporters began shouting questions, trying to be heard over one another, but Seth skillfully selected one by pointing and making eye contact with them.

"Why were these people selected for deportation?" the reporter asked.

Seth replied, "I can only speculate, but I believe it was because of their religion."

"Aren't there laws against religious persecution?"

"Yes, that is made quite clear in the Constitution."

Mia and I noticed Elsa Nordstrom among those trying to get a question in. She was a feature reporter for the local NBC affiliate that Mia and I usually watched. Elsa and I had crossed paths on the "nurse murder" cases the previous fall. When Seth called on her, she asked, "Where were they being held when you found them?

"Well, they were actually located by a private detective, Dan Burnett, and an associate. But to answer your question, they were found at a prison in Florida."

"Would they have been deported if he hadn't found them?" Elsa asked in a follow-up.

"Yes, *that* we are certain of."

More questions, similar in nature, were asked for the next ten minutes. When Seth stepped away from the microphone, the crowd remained, waving their handmade signs and continuing to chant.

During a lull in the action, the networks gave us background information about Judge Kennedy. We learned that, although unrelated to former President Kennedy, he was appointed by President Clinton in 1998. With twenty-seven years of service, he was considered a constitutionalist, with a strong record of his decisions holding up under appeal.

Later that morning, the detainees entered through a rear entrance and sat for their interviews with ICE agents, with their attorneys present. In some cases, they were represented by Seth. When it was all over, ICE chose not to press charges, and there were no hearings—everyone was able to go home early that day.

Game, set, match as far as the immigrants were concerned.

**At some point** in the afternoon, I received a call from Elsa: "So, Dan, you're quite the hero again."

"Thanks, Elsa, but I wasn't the only one. We had a couple of attorneys, some local PIs, and a tenacious husband involved. It took all of us."

"I'd love to get a chance to sit down with you to hear more."

"I assume you mean on camera?"

"Of course," she replied.

"Let's let this cool off a bit. But when I do any interviews, I promise you'll be the first one."

"I'm going to hold you to that, Dan."

"I have no doubts that you will."

# CHAPTER 13

While the Muslim detainees returned to their normal lives, or as normal as they could now be, it was a different case altogether for me and Colonel Wilkinson. We faced a slew of charges ranging from hijacking, theft of government property, interfering with a legal proceeding, aiding and abetting, and on and on. We had the proverbial book thrown at us, were arrested, handcuffed, and subjected to a mugshot that was released to the media.

After we spent a night at the Metropolitan Detention Center in Brooklyn, Seth managed to negotiate a bond of only $100,000 for each of us, which was posted by the ACLU. Although we were free for the time being, the charges were serious, and Seth had his work cut out for him.

This was all very upsetting for Mia, especially seeing me cuffed and perp-walked on TV. It proved her point about the dangers of how I'd been living my life. When I came home from my night in jail, she invited Hannah for dinner. While I was always thrilled to see my daughter, I knew they were about to gang up on me.

While Mia was preparing dinner, Hannah and I sat in the living room with a glass of chardonnay. She focused her crystal blue eyes on me and asked, "So, Dad, how did you feel about being perp-walked on television?"

"About how you would imagine a former cop would feel. How did you feel about it?"

Leaning forward in her chair, she replied, "I was horrified, and so was Mom."

"I'm sorry about that, Han. I suppose people were calling you both, asking if it was really me?"

"Yeah, that didn't bother me, though. I was more concerned about you."

"Listen, between that and scaring Mia, I've been doing some soul searching about my line of work. I realize I need to tone it down from now on."

Resting back in the chair, Hannah said, "I'm glad you're realizing that, Dad. You know you're my hero for rescuing me from those crooked cops—you saved my life. But it could have been you who was killed."

"I have no regrets about that one, Han. I'd do it again tomorrow if you were in danger. In a heartbeat."

"I know, and I appreciate that. But hijacking an airplane?"

"Look, I get it. But those were good people, who may have never been heard from again. We could not let that happen."

Hannah swirled the wine in her glass while thinking. "I know you couldn't, Dad. I guess I'm just asking you to be careful—reel it in a bit. Or maybe a lot. Mia needs you, and I need you." She reached for my hand and squeezed it.

"I promise I will."

A moment later, Mia stepped around the corner and announced, "Dinner is ready."

As we made our way into the kitchen, I noticed Mia stroke Hannah's back as she went by. That evening, she served us Caesar salad and shrimp scampi with fresh Italian bread. It was marvelous, of course. I could live off dipping the bread in scampi butter.

**THE NEXT DAY,** Seth requested a meeting with Joe and me in his office.

"How are you guys doing?" he asked, smiling.

Joe replied first, "Good, for the most part. Ariana was more exhausted than I was, but I've been getting reacquainted with the kids while she catches up on her sleep. I've also been keeping my eye on her for signs of trauma, but she's pretty tough."

Seth then turned to me.

"Mia and Hannah gave me some heat for the risks I took. Let's just say I'm making some adjustments," I said.

"That's good to hear. I'm sure they're right." Seth looked me in the eye before glancing at a legal pad. "Okay, here's why I called you in today: While I'm willing to represent you both, there are several reasons why you might want to have separate counsel, and at some point, it may become necessary. If so, I can recommend another attorney."

Joe and I nodded.

"So far, our public opinion campaign has been effective. Going forward, I'd like to have you do some television interviews, either separately or together. Joe, you with Ariana would make for a great interview. I've already begun discussions with *60 Minutes*."

Again, Joe and I nodded.

Seth continued, "I'm sure you've seen the benefits of having the court of public opinion on our side, and we need to keep it that way. I don't want to give the government any opportunity to make inroads with the public. With persistence, time will be on our side, and we'll work to appeal and delay at every opportunity. The President has demonstrated over the last several years just how effective that tactic can be. Who knows, the next administration may drop the charges altogether."

"You've handled this perfectly, Seth. Ariana and I would be happy to do some TV interviews," Joe offered.

"Great. Paula will organize a schedule for you. How about you, Dan?"

"Sure. I know Jim will welcome any PR we can get. We're still getting inquiries after chasing down the 'nurse murderer' in the Pacific Ocean."

Joe looked at me with raised eyebrows. "That was you?"

Seth replied for me, "It was—the media loved that one."

I shook my head, recalling how that went down.

"Okay, Paula is now your PR agency," Seth laughed.

**WHILE DRIVING TO** Mamaroneck, I thought more about my confrontation with Mia and Hannah. While I agreed that I needed to change my behavior for safety's sake, none of those dangerous situations were apparent when I first took the cases. The danger presented itself after I was involved, so I needed an indicator for when to back off. One that immediately came to mind was when I thought I'd need a gun. As I thought more about the past year, one stood out—

Hannah's kidnapping. If something like that ever happened again, all bets were off.

**On Sunday, Mia** and I tuned into *60 Minutes*. We watched as Ariana and Joe sat down with Leslie Stahl and told their story. Joe was in uniform and talked about how important Afghans like Ariana were to the war effort. They relived the panic on the ground as the American military prepared to depart Afghanistan, while the producers showed file footage of that chaos, with people clinging to the wheels of airplanes as they prepared to depart. Then they got into her experience as a prisoner of Immigration enforcement.

Ariana told the nation how she and her children were snatched off the street, and how they and the others were held at three different prisons, being moved each time in the middle of the night to avoid a legal proceeding. She recounted her fear when she was blindfolded while restrained by handcuffs and shackles. It was the highest-rated *60 Minutes* episode of the year.

As promised, my first interview was with Elsa Nordstrom. She thought doing the interview in the cockpit of my boat would make a compelling backdrop. The following afternoon, she and her crew arrived at the docks and took over.

As always, Elsa made a great appearance in front of the camera—blonde, pretty, with Nordic features. And she made me comfortable in front of the camera, too. She had done her research and knew all the right questions to ask, and managed to elicit some emotions from me as well. While I made sure to talk about returning the Muslim detainees to their families, she steered the conversation toward flying away in the plane with them in it. By the end of the interview, we'd both achieved our goals.

I also appeared on a few local news programs and the major networks' Sunday morning shows, reliving our efforts to locate the detainees when they were secretly moved out of state. As I expected, Jim was delighted with the public relations opportunities to promote our investigation business.

Up until that point, the Department of Justice had left us alone, as the administration focused on other issues. But a few weeks later, the President's public opinion poll numbers sank to an all-time low, and he felt he needed to go into "big bully mode" and rile up his base. He ordered the Attorney General (from Florida, of course) to hold a press conference and announce new charges against me and Joe. The charges were "conspiracy" and "impersonating an officer". In Joe's case, he'd worn his uniform while retired, which he *knew* was allowed, and as for me, I'd impersonated a prison guard.

Seth called me within a few minutes of the presser's conclusion. "Don't be overly concerned about the new charges, Dan. That was just an opportunity to generate media coverage and shift the focus away from the sagging polls. The original charges have more teeth, and we'll remain focused on those. I'll be making this same call to Joe."

"All right, Seth. Thanks for the call."

Later that afternoon, just in time for the evening news, Seth held a press conference with Joe and Ariana by his side, in front of their home. With Joe in street clothes and Ariana wearing a conservative dress, she held onto Joe's arm while Seth spoke to the media.

"Good afternoon, everyone," Seth began. "Thank you for your interest. I assume most of you have followed the story of this mother of two standing beside me, as she was held prisoner and threatened with deportation until her husband rescued her. What you saw today from the Attorney General was another attempt to demonize this family. This entire event was brought about by the administration's zeal to harass people of the Muslim faith. What man among us would not have done what Colonel Wilkinson did to rescue his wife from such grossly misguided authority?"

It was then that Katie came out of the house and hugged her father's leg. She was followed by Joey, who ran like a toddler toward Ariana's waiting arms. The image on the screen was of a family that anyone would have sympathy for.

"I ask anyone who is watching, do these people look like criminals? Do they look like gang members? This man, alongside me, took an oath to the Constitution and served his country for twenty years. He fought our enemies in Iraq and Afghanistan. Should he now have to fight his own government?"

Once again, Seth had won the day.

# CHAPTER 14

Jim and I were in the office working on some abstracts of title for our car collector clients before an upcoming auction in Scottsdale. While it was repetitive work for the most part, it kept me from dwelling on my legal troubles. If the weather had been cooperative, I would have gone sailing.

A call came in on the landline, and I answered, "Abbott and Burnett Investigations."

In broken English, a female voice asked, "Can you help me find my husband?" The accent sounded Spanish, which, in my years with the NYPD, I had barely learned enough to get by.

"Perhaps, Ma'am. Tell me what happened."

"Hector work yesterday and never come home. I saw news last night day laborers arrested at Home Depot. I'm afraid it was him."

"Where are you, Ma'am?"

"My home, in Port Chester."

"Would you like me to come to your home so you can tell me about it?"

"Si, I mean, Yes. You do that?"

"Yes, ma'am. If you tell me your address, I can come by this afternoon."

"Oh, thank you, sir."

After reciting her name and address, we agreed on 2:00.

Jim, having overheard me, asked, "What was that about?"

"Her husband is missing; she thinks he might have been one of the day laborers picked up at the Home Depot in Port Chester yesterday."

"It seems like the PR is working already." Jim smiled.

"That could be. How's your Spanish?"

"Decent. Working in the South Bronx all those years, it was a necessity."

"How would you like to take a ride to Port Chester with me?"

"Sure, whatever we have going on here can wait."

"Thanks, we'll stop for lunch on the way."

WE ARRIVED AT the address right on time. It was a two-family house in a neighborhood of older homes. While the homes appeared well-cared for, it was obvious that most of them had been covered with aluminum or vinyl siding at some point over the years. Like many houses of this vintage, when they were re-sided, the original ornamental woodwork and window trim were covered over, leaving them void of character. We took a moment on the sidewalk to imagine what the homes looked like fifty or a hundred years ago.

After climbing a few steps onto the front porch, we were greeted by a young woman in her twenties. "Ms. Martinez?"

"Yes, but you're here for my mother. She's expecting you and asked me to come over to help with the language. Please come in. I'm Olivia."

While she held the screen door open, Jim and I entered and were greeted by her mother. "Thank you for coming. I am Sophia Martinez," she said, offering her hand.

While shaking hands, I said, "I'm Dan, we spoke on the phone. This is my partner, Jim Abbott. He has better language skills than I do."

We followed her into the living room, where she gestured for us to sit. I guessed Sophia was in her late fifties, maybe sixty. She had a kind face with graying hair, pulled back in a bun at the nape of her neck.

"Okay," I began, "we've seen the reports on TV. Tell us about Hector."

"Would you like me to start, Mom?"

"Si, Olivia."

"My father left the house around 7:30 yesterday morning with our neighbor, Jaime. They're both carpenters. If they don't already have work lined up, they often go to Home Depot to look for work. Even if they already have a job, they might go there for materials they'll need that day."

"I'm familiar with the trades. So you think they were likely picked up in the raid?" I asked.

"We can't imagine any other reason why he didn't come home."

"Did Jaime make it home last night?"

"He does not come home either. I speak with Isabella, his wife," Sophia replied.

"Are you comfortable with English, Sophia? Jim can speak with you in Spanish if you prefer."

"English is good. Olivia will help if I no understand."

"Good. That will be easier for me," I chuckled, getting a smile from her.

"Would you like to tell me where you are from, and how you came here?"

Olivia spoke up, "Maybe I should tell the story, Mom. We arrived here in 2004, from Guatemala, when I was three years old. My mother and father did not want me to grow up there. They always said, 'In America, there is freedom.' We walked for over a week through Mexico, carrying only one suitcase and a backpack, and crossed the border in Laredo, just as you see on TV.

"My father worked in Texas for a month before we took a bus to New York, ending up in Port Chester, where my father had a carpenter job lined up. At first, we lived in an apartment near the center of town. My parents both worked hard and saved their money. In 2009, when the real estate market crashed and no one could get a mortgage, they got a good deal on this house because they could pay in cash."

*"Deberías estar orgullosa!"* Jim said to Sophia.

Both Sophia and Olivia nodded and smiled. He told me later that he'd said, "You must be proud."

Sophia and Jim conversed in Spanish for a few moments until Olivia continued. "So, I'm what is referred to as a dreamer. My father was able to obtain a work permit and temporary resident status through an employer he'd worked for. He has a Social Security number and pays withholding taxes, as do I, but my mom is unknown to the government." She nodded to Sophia, who smiled in return.

"Thank you, Olivia, that's a compelling story," I said. "But it sounds like your parents could be deported at any time."

"Probably so, and maybe me, too. I've been very afraid since this president took office."

"So, most importantly, we need to find your father. Do you know anyone else who was detained?"

Sophia answered, "No, just Jaime."

Jim had been taking notes and asked, "What is Jaime's last name?"

"Rodriguez," Sophia replied.

"It's most likely that Hector and Jaime are being held at a detention facility nearby. First, we'll try to locate him, and we'll also speak with an attorney who is familiar with Immigration issues."

"We might not be able to afford an attorney," said Olivia. "Can I ask what you charge?"

"Our usual fee is $85 an hour plus expenses, but don't worry about it just yet. We won't charge you anything until we know if we can help you."

Sophia understood enough to nod and smile.

"Is there anything else you can tell us that might help?" I asked.

"My dad has a truck, but we don't know where it is. I searched at Home Depot last night, but didn't see it."

"Does he have a driver's license?"

"Yes, he and I got them in 2019, when the State of New York passed a law allowing undocumented immigrants to apply."

"I recall when the law changed. Do you have the plate number?"

"He keeps the registration in the truck, but I found the title and the insurance card in his files. The plate number is on the insurance card." Olivia handed me copies, along with her contact information.

As we rose to leave, I said, "We'll start looking into this right away, and you'll hear from us by tomorrow at the latest."

When Sophia thanked us, Jim replied, *"Encantada de conocerte."*

They both smiled as we went down the steps. "Was that 'Pleased to meet you'?"

"It was."

**WHILE DRIVING BACK** to the office, we discussed where to start. Jim asked, "Where did you find the Muslim detainees?"

"Orange County Correctional, but they spent the first night in the local police station."

"Well, here we are on the second day since they were apprehended. That might also mean Orange County."

"Let me call up there and ask for Hector Martinez," I said, reaching for my phone. When the call was answered, I said, "I'd like to speak with a prisoner there."

"I'm sorry, prisoner calls are over for the day."

"Can you at least tell me if he is there?"

"Name, please."

"Hector Martinez."

After a few moments, he replied, "There is no one here by that name." He hung up before I could ask anything else.

I told Jim, "He either isn't there, or they won't tell me. Seth was the one who found them before."

"Do you want to ask Seth to try?"

"Maybe, but he did the others pro bono. I'm not sure I want to ask him for more free work. Let me try Elsa Nordstrom first."

"The Swedish reporter you did the interview with?"

"That's the one—she's pretty sharp."

I scrolled through my contacts and placed the call. She answered, "Dan?"

"Hi, Elsa. What do you know about the immigrants who were picked up at Home Depot yesterday?"

"Funny you should ask, I'm doing a piece on that for the evening news."

"We may be able to help each other on this. I've just been hired to locate one of them, Hector Martinez. Any word on where they're being detained?"

"I've been getting stonewalled all day. I've called all the prisons, and they either claim they aren't there or just refuse to tell me."

"Yeah, I just called Orange County Correctional, and they claim they aren't there either. I asked for Hector by name."

"I was just about to call the ACLU. Maybe they have a clue," Elsa said.

"All right, I'll keep looking. I'll let you know if I learn anything."

"Likewise, Dan. I'm glad you called."

Jim overheard enough of the conversation to know that I'd struck out. Next, I punched in Seth's number.

"Hey, Paula, Dan."

"Hi, Dan, we've gotten good feedback from your appearances."

"Good to hear, is the big guy in?"

"Yup, I'll put you through."

A moment later, I heard, "Hey, Dan. Nice job on those TV spots."

"Thanks. How did you go about locating the Muslims the first time?"

"A lieutenant at the Ardsley police station told me that's where they went after being in their jail the first night."

"I see. I'm trying to find out where the Home Depot detainees from Port Chester are being held. No one even knows how many of them there are. I tried calling Orange County, asked for a man by name, and was told he wasn't there."

"Yeah, as you know, ICE is keeping this all on the down low. Try calling the Port Chester Police. They might know something."

"Okay, Seth. Thanks."

While Seth was helpful, he didn't offer to do my job for me. From my days with the NYPD, I recalled working with Detective Mike Ryan in Port Chester. He was my next call.

"Police," was the abrupt greeting.

"Detective Ryan, Please."

"You mean, Inspector Ryan? I'll put you through."

I guess he'd been promoted since we last spoke.

"Ryan."

"Hi, Mike, Dan Burnett calling. We worked a case together a few years back, when I was at Precinct 49."

"Yes, Dan, I remember. How have you been?"

"I'm retired. Now I'm a PI."

"Good for you; I've got four more years. What can I do for you?"

"I'm trying to locate the immigrants picked up at the Home Depot yesterday."

"They were never here. The Chief didn't want anything to do with it."

"Do you have any idea where they might be detained?"

"Probably either Orange County or Batavia."

"Batavia. Is that up near Buffalo?"

"Between Buffalo and Rochester—about a five-hour drive."

"Okay, I appreciate your help, Mike."

"Take care, Dan. I'll let you know if I hear anything."

By the time we returned to the office, it was the end of the day. "Let's think on this overnight, Jim. We'll put our heads together in the morning."

"Okay, bud. Talk to you then."

While driving to Mamaroneck, I became increasingly pissed off at Orange County Correctional. I thought they'd lied to me about housing the detainees from Port Chester, and I knew they shipped the Muslims out in the middle of the night to avoid a hearing. I considered calling the ACLU to see if they had an attorney who would work with us, but looking at the clock, it would have to wait until morning.

When I arrived at Mia's, she was putting some hors d'oeuvres together on a small platter. "Hello, love. How was your day?" she asked, raising up on her toes to kiss me.

"Well, I've gotten myself involved with the detainees from the Home Depot."

She looked at me to see if I was serious. "Make us a cocktail and tell me about it."

"I'll make the drinks, but don't worry, there's no danger in what I'm doing."

"You're sure?"

"I'm sure."

"Good to hear, I'll carry out the snacks while you do that."

I chose to make Manhattans that night—sometimes there's just no substitute for bourbon. While mixing them, I realized how much these last few weeks had taken their toll on me. Between the events in Florida, the constant media attention, and now the Home Depot incident, I was tired. I hated to admit it, but at fifty-six, I no longer had unlimited energy.

When I delivered our cocktails, Mia raised her glass and said, "Cheers!"

"Cheers, sweetheart." I touched our glasses while sitting beside her.

Her hors d'oeuvre tray had baby quiches, little spring rolls, and a wedge of Gouda cheese. I popped a spring roll in my mouth.

"Did you have a difficult day, love?"

"Not really. I'm just tired. Tell me about yours."

"Well, we sent the holiday ball dress out for production today."

"That's an accomplishment! Good for you."

"Thanks. There was so much running around, I never had lunch. That's why I put these snacks together—I need something in my stomach before finishing this drink," she laughed.

"How about we go to the tapas place in town tonight?"

"I'd love to. Are you sure you're up to it?"

"I'm sure. Perhaps we could be seated at the banquette along the back wall again. We could get touchy-feely like the last time we were there." I smiled.

Her eyes met mine, and we kissed. Her kiss let me know she was on the same page. "Good, let's do it. I have an outfit that will be perfect!"

"I can't wait to see it."

"I'll go bathe, try to make a reservation for an hour from now."

"Okay."

She took the rest of her drink upstairs with her while I made the reservation. I continued to nurse my drink while watching the sky over the Sound turn orange ahead of the sunset. Anticipating my evening with Mia had completely changed my mood. I felt rejuvenated.

She came downstairs a while later with her hair styled in a formal manner, with a few strands falling alongside her face, and dangling earrings. The blouse she'd chosen was a deep purple, loose and flowing, with folds of excess fabric in lieu of sleeves. Her skirt was black, short, snug, and form-fitting, with a slit up one side. She also wore strappy black heels that accentuated her flawless legs.

"Wow, you look marvelous!" I exclaimed.

"I thought you'd like it. Shall we go?"

"Absolutely."

As we entered the familiar restaurant, we were met with the aromas of Spanish spices. The lighting was dim, and the decor was a rich combination of red and black, with matte gold accents, including the silverware—exactly as we remembered. We were seated where we had hoped, side by side along the back wall, where it was darker still. From there, we could see the whole restaurant. We ordered a pitcher of red sangria while we glanced at the menus, although we could have ordered from memory. After our wine was served, I asked our waiter to give us a few minutes before we placed our order.

Mia rested her head on my shoulder and said softly, "I love it here."

"And I love you."

Her lips found mine, and we kissed lightly, just barely touching, her tongue teasing my lower lip before sneaking inside. When we broke our kiss, she looked at me and smiled. "We have all night, love—I need to eat."

I motioned the waiter over and placed the food order out of memory: "Two orders of grilled octopus, an order of little neck clams, and a short rib empanada, please."

"Good choices, sir," the waiter said before heading to the kitchen.

Because it was tapas, we didn't know which would come first, but it didn't matter. After another sip of sangria, Mia took my hand and led it inside what served as a sleeve, but was just a side opening in the blouse, under her arm, and the folds of fabric. There, I found no undergarment of any kind; I had complete access to her body.

"My god, Mia. How do you expect me to make it through this meal?"

"Aroused, I presume," she laughed.

The clams were delivered first, and Mia dug right in. After eating a few, she slowed down and shared them with me from the same small plate. The rest of our order came out together, and the waiter placed an order of octopus in front of each of us, and the empanada in the middle.

"Can I get you anything else, sir?"

"Not right now, thanks."

We devoured the octopus; it was our favorite thing on the menu. It had been marinated and grilled, served with a mixture of sautéed baby potatoes, cherry tomatoes, Kalamata olives, and capers. There was also one hot pepper that flavored the dish, which neither of us dared cut into.

As delicious as the food was, I couldn't take my mind off the access I had inside Mia's top. She read my mind and smiled at me, knowing her tease was working. When we finished eating, the waiter took our plates away, and we remained at the table, sipping sangria with our fingers caressing each other's legs. While her hand was on my thigh, my fingertips were slowly working their way up the slit in her skirt. My caress became even lighter until I felt her leg shiver.

"I can't take much more of this, Dan. Can we go home?"

"Soon, sweetheart, soon."

**ON THE WAY** home in the car, I could no longer resist reaching inside her top, my fingertips tracing her curves, my touch tender and light as her breath quickened. When we arrived at her house, we began kissing in the car, this time with mounting passion. Once inside the house, we couldn't make it past the living room before yielding to our lust, still mostly dressed.

Momentarily gratified, we caught our breath before going upstairs, where I took a shower. When I came out, the bedroom was lit with candles, and Mia was lying naked on the bed, waiting for me. We again made love, this time patiently and tenderly in a variety of ways until we were thoroughly spent, falling asleep like two spoons together in a drawer.

# CHAPTER 15

I didn't get out of bed until 8:00, which was late for me. Mia had yet to stir. While making coffee, my mind went to Hector Martinez, my mission for the day. I knew his wife and daughter were expecting to hear from me. Along with my coffee, I sat down with my notepad and devised a plan to locate him. A few minutes later, I received a call from Mike Ryan, the police officer in Port Chester.

"Hey, Dan. You didn't hear this from me, but the driver who took the Home Depot immigrants to the detention facility was back at home in Port Chester within three hours. That rules out Batavia."

"It sure does, Mike. Thanks for that."

"He also said there were fourteen of them."

"All right, I owe you one."

"Enjoy your retirement."

I sent a text off to Jim with that information, then called Elsa.

"Good morning, Dan."

"Hi Elsa, did you have any luck with the ACLU?"

"They have an attorney assigned to the day laborers, but as of yesterday afternoon, he hadn't located them. My piece on the news last night was pretty weak; I had nothing to report."

"I hoped to catch it, but got involved with something else. Here's what I've learned: There are fourteen of them, and wherever they were taken was less than an hour and a half away."

"That narrows it down."

"Yeah, my money is on Orange County."

"That makes sense. Hey, would your clients be willing to do an interview?"

"They're here illegally. I'm sure they don't want to draw attention to themselves," I replied.

"That's been the case with everyone I've spoken to. Maybe we could do an interview in shadows, with their voices altered."

"Have you done that before?"

"Not yet, but the studio has the capability."

"All right, I'll ask my clients. Can you share the ACLU attorney's name with me?"

"Sure, I'll send you his contact information."

"Thanks, Elsa, talk to you soon."

While pouring a second cup, Mia put her arms around my waist from behind and hugged me. "Good morning, lover," she said with her head against my back, squeezing me.

"Good morning, sweetheart. How did you sleep?"

"Like a baby—I didn't want to get out of bed."

Nodding at the clock and smiling, I said, "I can see that."

She released me, heading for the coffee pot, wearing just an oversized T-shirt, her breasts swaying as she moved. *Why do I ever leave the house?*

"Are you working on the day laborers again today?" she asked.

"Yes. I'll find them today."

"That's positive thinking."

"Perhaps, but I will."

A few minutes later, while on my way to the office, I called the ACLU attorney, Justin Miles. After our greetings and introductions, I asked, "Have you spoken to Elsa this morning?"

"Not yet."

I told him what I'd learned from Mike Ryan and waited for him to comment.

"Thanks for that. They must be at Orange County Correctional."

"My thoughts exactly."

"I know some people in the public defender's office. I'll ask around and see if they can confirm that. I'll let you know if anything comes of it."

"Thanks, Justin."

When I arrived at the office, Jim was already there, watching the local news. Elsa was standing in front of Home Depot, reporting on the search for the day laborers. We continued watching as she interviewed tradesmen exiting the store, hoping for a sound bite.

Once her piece was done, Jim said, "So, you're thinking Orange County?"

"I am. I just spoke to an ACLU attorney. He's trying to confirm that."

"Shall we notify Olivia?"

"I suppose we should, but I'd like to get confirmation before we get their hopes up."

"Let's give it an hour, but we should call them this morning."

"Agreed."

While Jim and I put our heads together, trying to find a way to confirm they were in Orange County, Justin Miles called back. "Hi, Dan. There are two public defenders en route to Orange County at this time. They confirmed that the day laborers are there, and asked me to join them. Would you like to tag along?"

"For sure. Where are you?"

"White Plains."

"I'm in Scarsdale, do you want me to pick you up?"

"That would be great. Our travel reimbursements are a joke."

"I get it. Text me the address, and I'll text back my ETA."

"Okay."

I turned to Jim, "We just got confirmation. I'm heading up there now with an ACLU attorney."

"Do you want me to call Olivia?"

"That would be great. We should now be on the clock."

"I'll inform them. How about I suggest that they split our fee with Jaime's family?"

"That would certainly make it more affordable, and really, no more work for us. And tell them that it looks like an ACLU attorney will be representing the group."

"Good luck up there."


THE ACLU OFFICE was near the courthouse, just a block from Seth's office. A young Black man approached my car, and I assumed it was Justin. He was wearing a sport coat and slacks without a tie. Appropriate attire for an attorney, as of late.

On the ride up to Orange County Correctional, I learned that Justin had seen me doing television interviews and was thoroughly familiar with the Muslim case. "At our office, we're using your case as a model. The PR campaign your attorney is running has been executed perfectly. I'm sure they'll be teaching that in law school in no time."

I hadn't considered that previously, but he had a point. It *was* perfectly played. So far, at least, although I still faced serious charges.

We chatted along the way, mainly about the change in immigration enforcement over the last few months. As we entered the grounds of the Correctional Facility, which was in a field about a quarter mile from the road, Justin began texting. A few moments later, he announced that the Public Defenders were waiting for us inside the visitors' entrance.

We were greeted by a man and a woman, both young, recently out of law school. I knew the Public Defenders' office was where many young attorneys cut their teeth on their way to bright, lucrative careers. The woman introduced herself as Jennifer Baines, and the man, Aiden Moran. I thought to myself how trendy their names were. He was the first Aiden I'd ever met.

But they were both sharp. They'd already received a list of detainees, made copies for us, and had scheduled a meeting with them in a few minutes. Both Justin and I were impressed. The meeting would be held in the detainment ward's social room, as they were considered a low-security risk.

We did have to undergo thorough searches, however. And not just by walking through a magnetometer. We were each taken to a private room with a guard and asked to remove our clothing. Thankfully, it didn't include a cavity search, but they went through our clothing, looking for contraband.

Once we arrived in the social area, the detainees were delivered to us.

They were wearing prison-issued blue jeans, blue work shirts, and shower sandals; nothing that could be used as a weapon, or to hang yourself with.

Aiden asked each person to identify themselves, and as we went around the group, I noted Hector and Jaime. Jennifer asked each of them questions, guided by a form she was filling out. The questions primarily concerned how long they'd been in the country, whether they had a criminal record, and their immigration status. As defense attorneys, they would use this information to craft the best defense possible for their clients.

It took quite a while to complete the interviews, mainly due to language barriers, but Jennifer was very patient and put the men at ease. I was pleased to learn that neither Hector nor Jaime had a criminal record. Once completed, Aiden asked if Justin or I would like to speak. Justin asked about how they had been treated since being arrested. As I listened to their answers, no one had been beaten or abused, and they'd been fed two meals each day.

When it was my turn, I faced Hector and explained who I was, as well as the fact that I'd been hired by his wife and daughter. He seemed surprised, yet pleased to hear that. Jaime was sitting next to him, and I mentioned that I was there for him, too. I asked if they had any messages for their loved ones, and I gave each of them a notepad when they said they did. Their English was better than I expected, and I asked Hector where he'd left his truck. He told me it was at Home Depot, so I assumed it'd been towed.

While I was speaking with them, the attorneys answered questions from the others. Finally, Aiden told them that they would be representing them at an immigration hearing the following day, unless they had another attorney he could contact for them. No one spoke up.

As we left, I felt we had eased some of their fears. While I was happy to hear they had a hearing scheduled, I was concerned they'd be moved before then, like the Muslims were.

On the way back to White Plains, I asked Justin how he thought the hearing would go.

"They'll most likely be deported. They're either completely undocumented or their documentation has expired, as is the case with your clients. Only one of them claimed they'd been granted asylum, which the public defenders will verify this afternoon."

"Would it be safe for Hector's wife or daughter to attend the hearing?"

"Are they documented?"

"The wife, definitely not. But the daughter came here in 2004 when she was three, and calls herself a dreamer. She has a job, a Social Security number, and a driver's license."

"She'd be safe. The DACA act should protect her. Although, as you saw from the Muslims' case, this Department of Homeland Security thumbs its nose at the law. The hearing will be held at the Varick Street Immigration Court in Lower Manhattan. ICE agents are always there looking to arrest immigrants as they come and go for scheduled hearings. Anyone who thinks the immigration courts and ICE share the same goals is grossly mistaken.

"All right, Justin. I'll share that with my clients."

**AFTER DROPPING JUSTIN** off in White Plains, rush hour traffic was beginning to build, so I decided to head back to Mamaroneck and called Jim to bring him up to speed. He informed me that the Martinezes had approved our fee and suggested that I be the one to inform Olivia that I'd spoken with her father. I thought it best that I make the call after reaching Mia's.

When I entered the house, Mia was in the kitchen peeling potatoes.

"You're home early, love."

"Yeah, I was in the car most of the day and wanted to beat the traffic," I said as I kissed her neck from behind. "I have one more phone call to make, then I'll mix us a drink, if you're ready."

"I will be by the time you've made your call."

Once I was in the dining room at my "work station", I called Olivia.

"Hi, Dan. I had a nice conversation with Jim today in Spanish, mostly."

"I wish I could live up to that," I chuckled. "You'll be happy to know I saw your father today."

"Oh, that's so good to hear! Mom will be relieved. Where is he?"

"Where we thought, Orange County Correctional Facility. They all have hearings scheduled for tomorrow."

"Can I see him?"

"I discussed this with the ACLU attorney. He thinks it's safe for you to go because of DACA, but that's not 100% guaranteed. He is certain that Sophia should stay away. There's likely to be ICE agents there looking for family members, and we don't want her to be arrested, too."

"When and where tomorrow?"

"The hearings will be held at the immigration court on Varick Street in Manhattan, starting at 10:00, but with fourteen of them, I have no Idea how they'll schedule it."

"Okay, Mom and I will discuss it."

"I have a note from Hector and one from Jaime, too. Can I take a photo and text them to you?"

"That would be great."

"Give me a call in the morning and let me know your plans."

"I will, Dan. Thanks."

After sending the pictures to Olivia, I wandered back to the kitchen.

"What's your pleasure, sweetheart?"

Mia laughed, "My pleasure was last night!"

I grinned, "You know what I meant."

"You haven't made martinis in a while."

"Two Kettle One martinis coming up!"

After shaking up a batch with a touch of olive brine, I strained them into the appropriate glasses and dropped in an olive. "Cheers!" we both exclaimed in unison, before taking them to our happy place.

"I overheard you say you found the guys from Home Depot?"

"We did. They appear to be fine, and they have an immigration hearing tomorrow."

"How do you think that will go?"

"I hate to say this, but the attorney from the ACLU thinks it won't go well for most of them."

"They'll be deported?"

"Most likely. Currently, the Administration is only allowing undocumented agricultural and hospitality workers to stay. The President's big donor buddies threatened to shut off the money supply when he tried to deport their workers."

"So construction workers have to go?"

"It looks like it. They don't have enough big donors."

"That doesn't sound fair—what happened to an equal and fair justice system?"

"Unfortunately, that's an aspiration, not a reality," I said, shaking my head.

Slumping her shoulders, Mia said, "The whole thing is sad."

"I'm sorry, I didn't mean to depress you. Tell me about your day, sweetheart."

Shifting gears, she said, "Nothing too exciting in my world today, but lobsters were on sale at the grocery. I'm making us lobster rolls tonight, with potato salad."

"I don't think I've had a lobster roll since last summer. Out on the cape."

"Good memory—I think you're right."

# CHAPTER 16

Hector Martinez awoke in his cell in considerable pain. His back, which had been bothering him for the last few years, had suddenly gotten worse. Much worse. A year ago, a doctor at a walk-in clinic had ordered an X-ray and showed him what was wrong. The disc between two lumbar vertebrae had deteriorated over the years due to heavy lifting and working while bent over. Part of the disc was pressing against a nerve in his spinal column. The doctor told him he'd need to stop working like that, or it would get worse. But of course, he couldn't stop; if he didn't work, he didn't get paid.

His daughter, Olivia, bought him a quality orthopedic mattress for his sixtieth birthday, and it helped a lot. So long as he didn't lift heavy things by himself, he was okay. But these last two nights on a cheap prison bed had taken their toll. Hector couldn't find a position to relieve the pain that ran down his entire right leg. He found the only way he could sleep was on his knees in a fetal position with his butt in the air. Not really the way you'd want to sleep in a men's prison. Fortunately, his only bunkmate was his longtime friend, Jamie.

He'd tossed and turned all night, finding only brief periods of sleep in that fetal position. Knowing there was a hearing scheduled with an immigration judge that day, Hector wanted to be sharp and rested. The detective who visited him with the lawyers said his wife and daughter might attend the hearing. While he desperately wanted to see them, he was equally afraid they'd be imprisoned or deported, too.

With no access to even an Advil, when Hector could no longer take the pain, he climbed out of bed and stood in a corner. While standing relieved the worst of it, the corner kept him upright when he dozed for short periods.

Sophia Martinez also slept fitfully that night. She woke that morning, excited that her husband would have a hearing, but she was also afraid of what the outcome would mean for them. She'd hoped to attend the hearing, but Olivia had told her she couldn't go, or she'd risk being deported too. Her daughter was smart—she'd gone to school and gotten good grades, good enough to get a partial scholarship to college. She had a good job, one that paid a higher wage than her father's. She also had her own apartment and a reliable car. Coming to America was the right thing for Olivia. She was the reason they came.

While Sophia had her morning tea, she imagined all the possible outcomes. If Hector were allowed to stay, life would continue as usual. But if he were deported back to Guatemala, Sophia decided she would go with him. They'd been together since they were teenagers, and a life without her husband would mean nothing.

**AFTER THINKING ABOUT** it overnight, Olivia Martinez was determined to attend the hearing. She thought about what she'd wear to avoid looking like an immigrant and picked out her best business attire, which she'd worn on her last job interview—the one that got her the job at the bank. Having already arranged for the day off, Olivia called Dan and told him her decision.

"All right, do you know where it is?" he asked.

"I have the address, I'll ride the train into the city."

"Take the number one subway to Canal Street. It's a short walk from there. I plan on going myself, so look for me when you arrive—we'll sit together."

"Thanks, I'd like that."

After breakfast, she took her time getting dressed. While there was nothing she could do about her dark hair, she wore a hint of makeup, put on a white, feminine blouse, a charcoal skirt suit with stockings, and high heels. Looking into the mirror, she decided a pair of fashionable glasses would complete the look, and dug a pair out of her drawer. While she didn't need them to see, she had bought a cheap pair for just such an occasion. Glancing again at herself in the mirror, Olivia thought a thin briefcase would complete the look. She'd say she was a law student if anyone asked.


**AT 8:00 A.M.** sharp, after being restrained in handcuffs and shackles, Hector boarded the bus for the hearing. He was already nervous about what this day had in store for him, and sitting with Jaime, they barely spoke on the way into the city. Every time the bus went over a bump, pain would shoot down his leg. Looking out the window, he wondered if this would be the last time he'd see the country he had called home for twenty-one years.

**BEFORE THE PROCEEDINGS** started, Dan found Olivia outside the courtroom. "Did you have any trouble getting here?"

"None at all. Thanks for the tip about the subway."

"Come with me; I'll acquaint you with the attorneys—the good guys."

Dan introduced Olivia to Justin, Jennifer, and Aiden. They were exceptionally gracious, and Justin, knowing the risk she was taking, said, "I'm glad that you came. Please sit in the row directly behind me, alongside Dan. Your father will be able to see you there."

"Thank you."

Then they all filed into the courtroom, and once seated, the bailiff opened a side door and led the detainees in. Olivia was shocked to see her father in restraints, and tears flowed down her cheeks. Dan reached for her hand, holding it to comfort her. Hector's eyes searched the courtroom, and when he saw Olivia, he nodded to her and mouthed "I love you," with moisture pooling in his eyes.

"All rise," the bailiff instructed.

When Judge Pendergast was seated, everyone took their seats.

"Would counsel approach the bench?"

All the attorneys scurried forward and stood before the judge. Olivia whispered, "What are they saying?"

"I'm not sure. Maybe he's explaining his rules."

Once the attorneys retook their seats, Judge Pendergast asked the government prosecutors to present their case for each detainee individually.

Josh Volpe, the lead prosecutor, announced, "Your Honor, for the record, each of these men was apprehended by Immigration and Customs Enforcement agents in Port Chester, New York, on May 10th of this year. The first case today is Carlos Santos."

When the bailiff motioned for him to stand, Josh continued. "Mr. Santos has been in this country illegally for at least ten years. He works as a day laborer near Port Chester and has no criminal record. When asked to provide any immigration documentation, he had none."

The judge then said to Aiden Moran, "Counsel, do you have anything to say on Mr. Santos' behalf?"

"I have no evidence to dispute anything Mr. Volpe has said so far today. But I would like the court to be aware that Mr. Santos has a wife and family here, and his children are United States citizens. As Mr. Volpe stated, he has no criminal record, and he provides for his family, Your Honor."

The judge then asked, "Mr. Santos, would you like to address the court?"

"I would just like to say, 'I love America.'"

"Thank you, sir."

"Next, Mr. Volpe."

"Your Honor, next we have Jaime Rodriguez. He's employed as a carpenter in Port Chester, New York. He has been in this country for twenty years. At one time, he had a work permit and was granted temporary citizenship. But those have since expired. He has a wife and family here, and has no criminal record, Your Honor."

"Mr. Moran, your turn."

"Your Honor, I have no evidence to dispute anything Mr. Volpe has told you about Mr. Rodriguez. But I would like the court to be aware that Mr. Rodriguez owns his own home, and his son is enlisted in the United States Marine Corps. As Mr. Volpe stated, he has no criminal record, has steady work as a carpenter, and provides for his family."

The judge said, "Mr. Rodriguez, would you like to address the court?"

"No, Your Honor."

"Next, Mr. Volpe."

Realizing her father was next, Olivia squeezed Dan's hand.

"Your Honor, now we have Hector Martinez. He's also employed as a carpenter in Port Chester, New York. He has been in this country for more than twenty years. At one time, he had a work permit and was granted temporary citizenship. But both of those expired in 2019. He has a wife and family here. He also has no criminal record, Your Honor."

"Mr. Moran?"

"Your Honor, I have no evidence to dispute anything Mr. Volpe has told you about Mr. Martinez. However, I would like the court to be aware that Mr. Martinez also owns a home here. As Mr. Volpe stated, he has no criminal record, has steady work as a carpenter, and provides for his family without any government assistance. Like many of the others, Mr. Martinez has been a model member of the community, and removing him will be a major disruption to his family."

"Mr. Martinez, do you have anything to say to the court on your own behalf?"

Standing, Hector said, "Your Honor, I came to this country twenty-one years ago. I work hard, and I own my own home. Nowhere else but America could I have done that. Thank you, Your Honor."

"Next, Mr. Volpe,"

It went on like this for another hour. None of them had legal residency, whether temporary or permanent. Even the man who claimed he'd been granted asylum could not provide any proof of that, and neither could the defense team, despite an exhaustive search.

When all the cases had been presented, Judge Pendergast addressed the courtroom. "I'm prepared to rule: In each of these cases, the testimony shows that these men are in this country unlawfully. Up until this year, if an undocumented immigrant proved to be a contributing member of the community, I could use my discretion to allow them to stay and help them obtain documentation, or perhaps citizenship. However, it is no longer up to me to decide who stays and who must go. I must find for the prosecution, and order these men to remain in custody pending deportation to their countries of origin. Any place other than their country of origin will require approval by this court. This hearing is adjourned."

Olivia shuddered and began sobbing, clinging to Dan's arm. Everyone at the defense table turned to her, offering condolences. When people began filing out, Dan and Justin noticed ICE agents standing in the lobby. Justin said, "You two follow me."

He led Dan and Olivia to a conference room with its own exit, not to the lobby. Moments later, the three of them were outside on the street.

"Thank you for this," Dan said, shaking Justin's hand.

"We don't need any more drama today," Justin replied.

Olivia was not too upset to realize what Justin had done for her as Dan led her to the subway station. He rode with her in silence to Grand Central Station, where he asked, "Are you taking the New Haven Line?"

"Yes," she replied, slightly disheveled, still dabbing at her eyes.

"Good, I'll ride with you as far as Mamaroneck."

Once they found two seats together, Olivia used a compact mirror to fix her makeup and hair, then asked, "Should I not have been hopeful?"

"You should always be hopeful. While the ruling didn't go the way we wanted, it didn't surprise me. This new administration is focused on deportations. At least they had due process."

Olivia had no reply.

"Do you know what your mother's plans are?"

"We haven't discussed it, but I can't imagine her not wanting to be with my father."

"I can understand that. If she'd like some help with her decision, let me know. Justin might be able to explain her options."

Olivia nodded. Dan's stop was before hers, and as he rose to get off, Olivia hugged him and said, "Thank you for looking out for me today."

"It was my pleasure. Good luck, Olivia."

# CHAPTER 17

By the time I reached Mia's, I was starving. After a kiss and a hello in her office, I made myself a sandwich and sat down to review my voicemails. There were two requests from Elsa for a callback. I punched in her number.

"Dan, I saw you in the courtroom, but you never came out."

"Sorry, Elsa, I went out a different exit with the attorneys."

"Was that the immigrant's daughter you were with?"

"It was. She was pretty upset, and I didn't want her to face the crowds."

"Do you mean the media, or ICE?"

"Both, but ICE was the main reason."

"What did you think of the verdict?"

"It didn't surprise me. I was happy there was a hearing, though, due process and all that."

"Yeah, I suppose you're right. Any comment for the record?"

"No, sorry, Elsa."

"Okay, look for me tonight on the news!"

"I'll be watching."

There was a certain give-and-take with Elsa. I thought about it for a moment and decided I was okay with it. So far, it had been beneficial for both of us. My other voicemails were junk, so I called Jim to check in.

"Hey, buddy. I saw the verdict on TV. Was Olivia upset?"

"She was, but I managed to get her out of there without facing ICE."

"Good. We're still getting calls from immigrant families. Do you want to handle the replies?"

"Why don't you take them? I could use a break."

"All right, I'll follow up."

"Thanks. We'll talk soon."

LATER THAT EVENING, Olivia called: "Do you think it would be safe for me to visit my father at the prison?"

I thought for a moment and replied, "Probably. I haven't seen ICE there during my other visits."

"Good. I called up there, and visiting hours are between 10:00 and 4:00. I was thinking of going up in the morning, before he's shipped out."

"Do you want me to go with you?"

"No, that's okay. If I dress the way I did today, I don't think I'll look like an immigrant."

"I agree, you looked perfect today. Please call me when you arrive, and again when you leave. I'll be worried about you."

"I will. Thanks for your concern."

I hadn't said that lightly—I would be worried.

THE FOLLOWING MORNING, Mia was up and out early to catch a train to the city. She usually spent a day or two each week at the fashion design office she shared with her partner.

At 10:00 a.m., I received a call from Olivia, who told me she was about to enter the prison.

"Do you see any ICE vehicles in the parking lot?" I asked.

After a few moments, she replied, "None with markings that would identify them as such."

"All right, call me as soon as you leave."

"Okay, Dan."

It was my plan to take the day off and catch up with some things I'd been putting off. One of those was checking in with Joe and Ariana. She and I chatted for a bit, and it sounded like their life had returned to normal. When Joe came on the line, we talked about our legal issues. We didn't have any court dates pending, but we didn't know if that was due to Seth's efforts or the slow, grinding wheels of justice. Before ending the call, we discussed getting together some-time, and he mentioned that they wanted to meet Mia.

An hour later, Olivia called: "I'm so glad I got here early; Dad told me they're being deported today on a flight to Central America, stopping in Guatemala and Honduras."

"How is he?"

"He looked fine, but told me his back was acting up again. As happy as he was to see me, he's more concerned about my Mom."

"Has she made any decisions?"

"Not yet. She's waiting to hear about Dad from me, and he said he'd call her when he reaches Guatemala."

"Does he have a place to stay?"

"His sister and my cousins are there. I'll call them this afternoon to tell them to expect him."

"And how about Jaime?"

"He has family there, too."

"Great, it sounds like things will work out."

"I hope so, thanks for everything, Dan."

"Bye, Olivia."

At noon, I stepped outside and saw it was a beautiful day. I spent the rest of it at the marina, successfully keeping my mind off the immigrant cases.


MIA AND I both arrived home at the same moment, just in time for happy hour. Since it was a Friday and the weather forecast was perfect, I suggested we spend the weekend on the boat.

"Sounds good to me!" she replied, taking a sip of a Cosmopolitan.

"I was at the marina this afternoon, and everything is ready to go."

"Do you want to invite Hannah?"

"Sure, I'll give her a call in a bit. How was your day in the Big Apple?"

"Too crowded. It was standing room only on the train."

"I'm sure. Traffic was brutal on the way back from City Island, too."

Mia hugged my shoulder and fantasized, "Maybe someday we can live on a tropical Island, with no trains and no cars."

"Or on a boat, in a secluded bay, on a tropical island."

"Mmm, that would be wonderful."

We spent the next several minutes snuggled in our happy place, dreaming of white sand, turquoise water, and tropical breezes.

**MIA AND I** spent the weekend on *Privateer*, and Hannah joined us on Sunday. The three of us sailed over to Oyster Bay and back. I was overjoyed to see Mia and Hannah's relationship grow deeper with each day they spent together. By the end of the weekend, I was so rested and recharged that I was considering taking on some of the immigrant cases that had been piling up.

However, on Sunday evening, I received an email from Seth, asking if I had time on Monday to meet in his office along with Joe. He mentioned that there had been some developments in our legal cases, and he wanted to discuss our strategy. So much for rested and recharged.

# CHAPTER 18

Seth arrived at his office early on Monday. He'd received notice on Saturday of a scheduled trial date for Joe and Dan. Sometimes these notices were just bluffs or maneuvers. But with the date just ten days away, he had to take them seriously. He'd emailed his clients on Sunday with some times he hoped they'd be able to come in. Joe's reply was anytime Monday, and Dan replied, "The sooner the better." Seth had them scheduled for 10:00 a.m.

When they arrived at Seth's office, Paula welcomed them into the conference room and served them coffee. They had been there often enough lately that she remembered how they took it. A minute later, Seth joined them along with another man. "I'd like you to meet a colleague of mine, David Weber."

During introductions and handshakes, David said, "Nice to meet you, gentlemen. Everyone calls me Webb."

Seth followed with, "I mentioned before that there may come a time when you would need separate counsel. That time has come. Please, let's sit."

Dan guessed that Webb was in his forties, and one feature that stood out was his full lips, somewhat unusual for a Caucasian.

"Seth has brought me up to date on your cases, and I read the history over the weekend," Webb informed them.

"Webb and I go all the way back to law school. I chose him for you, Joe, because of his experience in Military Law."

Joe looked at them both curiously. "So you're thinking this could lead to a court-martial?"

"That's a possibility. We aren't there yet, but we're covering all the bases. Perhaps just having Webb on board may deter them from going that route when the time comes. And if they do, you'll have excellent counsel."

Dan interjected, "Tell us more about this upcoming trial."

"At this point, there's a preliminary hearing scheduled for June 2nd, with Judge Stanley Ferris. I don't know him, but Webb has been in his courtroom before. Today, I'd like to discuss a strategy to steer this in a way most beneficial to us. I've already filed a motion to delay the hearing for thirty days so we have more time to prepare."

Dan and Joe settled into their chairs to listen.

Seth continued, "Webb and I agree that a trial by jury would be best for our case. With a jury trial, we'll be able to play to their emotions, in your case, Joe, your service to your country, and your need to protect your wife from an unlawful deportation when all legal options have failed. And in your case, Dan, we'll highlight your thirty years of service with the NYPD with a flawless record, and your recent fame from solving cases that the police and FBI could not."

Webb said, "The public opinion efforts will be crucial here. We want every potential juror already to have a favorable opinion of you before the trial starts."

"That implies this trial will go forward?" Dan quizzed.

"We'll be filing motion after motion as to why this case should be dismissed. We'll be challenging the evidence at every turn and throwing a wrench in the works at every opportunity," Webb replied.

Seth added, "The President gave us all a lesson in how to make a mockery of our judicial system over the last several years. Every attorney in the country is using those tactics."

"As the case progresses, we'll need to decide if it benefits you to be tried together or separately, and if a military or civilian trial favors you, Joe," Webb said.

"You can now see why you need separate counsel, right?" Seth asked.

"So we can throw each other under the bus?" Dan quipped, smiling.

"Not quite," Webb chortled. "That would unlikely benefit either of you."

"How are we paying you guys for all this?" Joe asked.

Seth responded, "Paula has set up a legal defense fund. We should get support from the ACLU and other pro-democracy groups. She'll start a GoFundMe page on social media, and several organizations support undocumented immigrants. I don't think you'll have to worry about money."

Dan and Joe looked at each other, expressing relief.

"Do either of you have questions, concerns, or anything to add?" asked Seth.

"I assume we'll be having more meetings like this?" Dan asked.

"You can count on that. But we'll keep you apprised over the phone for the most part."

With that, the meeting broke up with another round of hand-shakes. As Dan and Joe exited the conference room, Paula said, "I'll be scheduling more media interviews for you guys, so be ready."

In unison, they replied, "Thanks, Paula."

While riding the elevator down, Dan asked, "Do you have time for lunch?"

"Sure."

"Thai food?"

"Sounds good."

"I know just the place."

# CHAPTER 19

Later, while driving back to Mamaroneck, I received a phone call. Over the speaker, I heard, "Hi, Dan, it's Olivia. My mom's ready to talk about going to Guatemala."

Checking the time, I said, "I can be at her house in half an hour."

"Really? That would be great."

"Sure, I'm already in the car heading your way."

"Thanks, we'll be ready."

After thinking for a moment, I called Justin, the ACLU attorney.

"Good afternoon, Dan."

"Hey, Justin, Olivia's mother wants to go to Guatemala to be with her husband. What's the best way for her to do that?"

"She should take advantage of the self-deportation program. She'll get favorable treatment if she ever wants to come back. Or so they say."

"How does she go about doing that?"

"If you give me her contact information, I'll send her the instructions. It's pretty easy."

"Okay, thanks. We'll get that to you this afternoon."

"Good, happy to help."

When I arrived at Sophia Martinez's house, both she and Olivia welcomed me with open arms and hugs.

Sophia said, "Thank you so much for all you do for us. A life-saver...I got bill, you no charge for day in court?"

"No, I was there for my own curiosity."

"But you help Olivia."

"That was my pleasure."

While Sophia and I were having that conversation, Olivia served tall glasses of iced tea to everyone. We sat in the living room, chatting like old friends for a few minutes, then I said, "I called the ACLU attorney on my way here. He says there's a self-deportation program that you should take advantage of before going to Guatemala."

Olivia asked, "Justin?"

"Yes."

Olivia explained to her mother how he had helped her avoid ICE on the way out of the courtroom.

"He said to forward your contact info, and he'll send you the instructions. Maybe you should contact him, instead of me, that way you'll have an open line of communication," I said.

"I'll do that today."

I handed her one of Justin's cards, and while sipping tea, I asked if they'd spoken to Hector.

"Yes," Sophia replied. "It good to hear voice. We very happy speaking."

Olivia then added, "He's safe and sound at his sister's house. The plan is for me to sell this house and send them the money. Between that and their savings, they should live very well in Guatemala."

"That's good to hear. Since you work in a bank, I assume you know how to send the money safely?"

"Of course. Mom will open a bank account when she gets there, and I'll wire the funds directly."

Fearing I had questioned her expertise, I said, "Excellent. It sounds like you have it all figured out." Rising to leave, I said, "Good luck to you, Sophia. Give Hector my best."

"I will. Thank you," she said, hugging me again.

"Yes, thank you for everything, Dan. I'll let you know how it all works out."

"I'd like that, Olivia."

I MADE IT back to Mia's in time for happy hour. While enjoying our cocktails, I told Mia all about my meeting with the lawyers and the upcoming hearing.

"Could you go to prison over this?" Mia asked, concerned.

"It's a possibility, but I have the best lawyer around, and we have a well-thought-out plan."

"I hope so."

Hugging her, I said, "Don't worry, sweetheart, I'm not worried." In actuality, I *was* fearful, but didn't want Mia to see it.

While she was cooking dinner, I received a call from Paula: "Can you make it into the city tomorrow afternoon? Nicolle Wallace would like to have you and Joe appear on *Deadline: White House* at 4:00."

"I can."

"Good. I'll call Joe and confirm it with you tonight."

"Okay. Paula. I guess Round Two begins now."

"That's right, here we go again."

On the evening news, Mia and I saw a clip of the Attorney General holding a press conference, stating that they would hold Joe and me accountable to the full extent of the law. This upset Mia all the more, and I saw her eyes well up.

With my arm around her, I explained, "This is just them playing to their base and posturing for the public—they're trying to get ahead of the media show that we'll be doing, starting tomorrow."

Mia remained silent, holding back tears. My explanation didn't seem to placate her much.

Later, after dinner, Elsa Nordstrom called: "Hey, Dan. I saw the AG's Press conference. Would you like a chance to respond?"

"I would, but I'm pretty well booked for tomorrow. How about the following day?"

"I'd really like to get you on tomorrow, while you're in the spotlight. What if I come to you?

I wondered if Nicolle Wallace would think I was stealing her thunder if I interviewed with Elsa before her. "When would it air?" I asked.

"Between 6:00 and 6:30, on the local news."

"Okay. I can come to your studio at 1:00 or so, if that works for you."

"Great, thanks, Dan. See you then."

During our conversation, it occurred to me that they were both at the NBC studios in Rockefeller Center. I could go a little early, interview with Elsa, then sit with Nicolle, whose show was live. I also didn't want to invite Elsa to Mia's house. Mia had previously shown a hint of jealousy toward her, and I knew to respect that. Additionally, this was our sanctuary. There was no way I wanted any media in the house.

IN THE MORNING, when I checked in with Jim regarding the new immigrant cases, he said, "I met with two of the families yesterday. One of them is a waiter in Larchmont, and the other is a landscaper. I discovered they're being held at the facility in Brooklyn, and neither can make bail. After speaking to their families, it will be difficult for us to get paid."

"I'll give you the names of a couple of public defenders," I offered. "Have the families contact them. Perhaps they'll take their cases and negotiate a bail amount they can afford."

"Okay, shoot."

After I read the names and phone numbers to Jim, he said, "I'm doing TV interviews today. I'll be in tomorrow if nothing else gets scheduled."

"I hope you can come in," Jim laughed. "The phone will be ringing off the hook after those interviews air."

"All right, man. Talk to you later."

On my way out the door, I stopped in Mia's office and kissed her goodbye. "I'll be on *Deadline: White House* this afternoon if you care to watch. I doubt I'll be home before 6:00."

"I'll be watching, love. Text me your ETA, and I'll have a Manhattan waiting for you."

"I will. Thanks, sweetheart."

Upon entering the NBC studios, I discovered that the network newsroom and the local news operations were located in separate areas. When I told the reception staff who I was here to see, they escorted me to the local newsroom.

The few interviews I'd done previously with Elsa were outside the studio, but I had an idea of what to expect and was comfortable with it. Before the crew arrived, a makeup artist brushed my hair and applied makeup so I'd look good on camera.

Elsa stepped onto the set, already with makeup, along with the camera crew. Someone set a mug of water next to me, and Elsa asked if I was ready.

I nodded, and the cameras began recording. She looked into one of them and began, "We're speaking with Dan Burnett today, who's becoming New York's hottest Private Investigator. You'll remember when he tracked down the 'nurse murderer' last fall, and just a few weeks ago, he found and returned a group of Muslims who were about to be unlawfully deported. Did I get that right, Dan?"

I smiled, nodded, and replied, "Pretty much, but I had some help."

"Tell us about the legal issues you're now facing."

I summarized the gist of it, and Elsa was already knowledgeable enough to ask some pointed questions that framed the prosecution in a negative light. They recorded about ten minutes worth, which I knew would be edited to less than four. When it was over, I felt I'd given her some good sound bites to work with and that I'd come across favorably to the viewers.

Done there, I wandered up to the MSNBC studios, fascinated by all the surroundings. The sets seen on TV were just a tiny part of the building. The rest looked like an electronics and costume warehouse. Once at MSNBC, I saw Joe had already arrived and was sitting for makeup. Gone was the uniform; he was in street clothes with a crisply starched shirt. We chatted for a few minutes before a producer came out and showed us some talking points that Nicolle would cover, explaining that she didn't want us to be taken by surprise.

Just before the show began, we were seated offstage so we could observe what was happening and become comfortable with the surroundings. Nicolle came by and introduced herself on her way to the set.

During the introduction, the lights went bright, and she began, "Hello everyone, we start today with breaking economic news." Then she proceeded with that piece of news and introduced her first guest, an expert on the economy and the Federal Reserve. After announcing a commercial break, the lights dimmed, the guest left, and we were ushered into seats adjacent to the host while she reviewed her notes and questions.

When the lights came back up, Nicolle introduced us before telling the viewers about our rescue mission in Florida, and then began her questions. Since we'd both been doing these interviews over the last month, we were comfortable in front of the cameras.

"Colonel Wilkinson, where would your wife be today if you hadn't rescued her?"

"In some foreign country, I'm sure. Maybe the prison in El Salvador—it's likely I might never know."

Like Elsa, before her, Nicolle didn't shy away from tough questions, but it was clear she viewed our ordeal as part of a troubling political trend—what some in the media had called "demonization for political purposes."

When it was done, we felt successful in our mission to curry favor with the public. We walked out together before going our separate ways; I headed to Grand Central, and Joe to the parking garage. Once on the train, I texted Mia my ETA, then sat back and relaxed. I'd been on my toes mentally all afternoon and looked forward to the Manhattan waiting for me.

# CHAPTER 20

When I walked into the house, Mia greeted me with a kiss, then poured two drinks from a chilled shaker. "Cheers. How was your day?"

"All went well. I think we accomplished what we wanted to."

"I saw you guys with Nicolle—both of you came across very well. By the way, after your segment was over, I switched over to Fox—they were showing a rerun of the AG from yesterday, followed by a legal expert discussing the severe penalties for hijacking."

Nodding, I said, "That's the way it will be until this is over—both sides fighting for the public's opinion. I wouldn't be surprised if they start taking polls."

"Polls to see which side is winning?"

"Something like that. I did another piece with Elsa Nordstrom. It should be on any minute."

"Let's watch," Mia said, moving toward the TV.

With Manhattans in hand, we sat down in front of the television, and Mia toggled the remote. The anchors teased the spot a few times before finally running it. We watched Elsa introduce me, highlighting my previous investigative successes before moving on to the issue at hand. I thought I came across well on camera, and

Mia watched the comfortable rapport between the two of us before commenting, "She has the hots for you, Dan."

"Huh? What do you mean?"

"I'm just sayin'. A woman can tell when another woman has a thing for her man, and I'm telling you to watch yourself around her. She's very attractive and used to getting what she wants," Mia stated, with a bit of fire in her eyes.

"I'll take your word for it, but I can tell you it's all business between us," I said, pulling her close.

"I know that you believe that, love, but she has other ideas."

Fortunately, my phone buzzed, and I welcomed the interruption. I heard Paula's voice. "Great job today, Dan. I saw both of your interviews, and they could not have gone better."

"Thanks. What's next?"

"You've got tomorrow off, but the next day I have you on the CBS morning show, and then on CNN's *Out Front*. The CNN show can be a video call, but unfortunately, CBS is live in the studio at 8:00 a.m."

I winced at the thought of catching a 6:00 a.m. train, but said, "Okay."

"Do you have a video set up at home?"

"Well, I can do Zoom."

"A computer camera isn't good enough—you'll look like you're underwater. How about if we do it in the conference room? We have a quality camera and the necessary lighting. CNN will pre-record the interview in the afternoon."

"That's fine with me. It'll save me an evening trip into the city."

"Good. You may want to consider setting up a studio in your home or your office. It will save you a lot of travel, and I'll be scheduling you daily for a while."

"Yeah, maybe I should," I replied.

"All right, I'll get back to you with a time to come in."

"Thanks, Paula. I'll plan to be at CBS before 8:00 tomorrow."

Mia had gone across the room to the kitchen and started preparing dinner while I was on the call. When it ended, she asked, "What was that all about?"

"It was Paula with my interview schedule for Thursday."

"Nothing tomorrow?"

"No. I promised Jim that I'd give him a hand with the immigrant cases. Since doing all these interviews, we've been getting a lot of calls."

"That doesn't sound too dangerous."

"Don't worry, sweetheart. I've come up with some rules about what to get involved with."

"Do tell."

"Well, first, if I'm considering bringing a gun, maybe I shouldn't get involved, and second, I shouldn't do anything that might be illegal."

"That's a good start. I could probably think of a few more."

"I'm sure. It's a work in progress."

"Glad to hear you've been thinking about it. How does Mexican food sound tonight? I came across an enchilada recipe that looks interesting."

"Sounds good to me."

THE FOLLOWING DAY, I went to the office in Scarsdale, where I found Jim already at his desk. "Hey, partner. Every time I turn on the TV, I see your face. That's some PR campaign you're running," he said.

"It's all Seth and Paula. They say this case will be won or lost by public opinion."

"That's probably true. Do you want a crack at some of these cases coming in?"

"Sure."

He handed me a list of recent phone calls, which included a few details: name, contact information, the person missing, and the duration of the absence. If a location was known, it was also noted.

After perusing the list, I said, "So our mission is to locate these people, and that's it?"

"Yeah. We can refer them to an attorney or suggest a next step, but we can't give legal advice."

"It was a lot of work finding the Muslims and Hector Martinez. How did you locate the people at the Brooklyn Detention Center so quickly?"

"I know a guard there. I paid him a hundred bucks to confirm the names."

"And we can keep doing that?"

"Sounds like it," Jim replied.

"It seems all the detainees are either at Orange County or Brooklyn Detention, at least so far. We need someone like that in Orange County. Just calling there and asking for a prisoner by name won't work, I've tried it."

"Any ideas?"

I explained to Jim how the PIs I'd hired in Florida and Texas had followed some guards after their shifts were over, and managed to get their cooperation. "What if I do the same?"

"Confidential informants. We used them all the time at the department," Jim conceded.

"All right, it looks like I'm heading to Orange County."

"Good luck, buddy."

**It took me** over an hour to get up there. When I did, I found an out-of-the-way spot to park with a good view of the employees' parking lot. I bided my time scrolling through my phone, returning emails and texts. Back in the day, I'd always have a newspaper to read on a stakeout, along with a thermos of coffee.

I hadn't been there long when I witnessed a changing of the guard, with vehicles entering and exiting the lot. Noticing a particularly beat-up car leaving, I followed it, assuming the driver was in need of some extra cash. About a mile from the prison, he stopped at a convenience store, and I parked alongside his car, waiting for him to exit. A minute later, he walked out with a fresh pack of Marlboros.

Now standing near his car, I said, "Excuse me, do you work at the prison?"

Glancing down at his uniform, he said sarcastically, "Gee, how could you tell?"

Chuckling, I said, "I'm wondering if you could use some extra cash?"

He looked at me suspiciously, but replied, "If this is about bringing in drugs, forget about it."

"No, no. I need a source inside the prison who can confirm if someone is being held there. It's worth a hundred bucks for a yes or no answer. This may be an ongoing arrangement."

He thought for a moment and said, "I can do that."

I handed him a C-note and said, "Good. The first name is Julio Ramirez."

"Yes, he's one of the people ICE brought in."

"When did he arrive?" I asked, checking to see if he was being truthful, and not just saying yes for the cash.

"He must have come in yesterday afternoon, because he wasn't there when my shift ended, but I saw him when I arrived this morning."

Knowing that fit the timeframe, I said, "That sounds right. How can I reach you with more names?"

"He pulled out his phone, and we traded contact information. I saw that his name was Robert Skinner, and he said, "Just text me."

"Thank you, Robert."

"Any time."

It was the middle of the afternoon when I returned to the office. I told Jim, "We now have a source at Orange County. Julio Ramirez arrived yesterday afternoon."

"Excellent. I'll notify his family."

"I can confirm more by just texting my guy, but our time on the clock won't add up to much."

"No worries. All our agreements have a $500 minimum plus expenses."

"That'll work. Who's next?"

"Check the list. I marked all the ones that are in Brooklyn."

A few moments later, I texted Robert two more names. He replied immediately that he'd let me know tomorrow.

Before calling it a day, I told Jim that I'd be tied up tomorrow with interviews, but could continue communicating with Robert via text.

"All right, partner. Good luck."

It began raining on my way to Mia's, and by the time I arrived, there were thunderstorms. We enjoyed our afternoon cocktails in our happy place, marveling at lightning bolts over Long Island Sound as thunder shook the house.

**I WAS UP** and out early to catch the 6:15 train into the city. After grabbing a cab at Grand Central, I arrived at the CBS West Side studios with time to spare. Again, like at NBC, I was escorted to the green room where I sat for makeup, and the hosts stopped by to introduce themselves during commercial breaks.

When it was my turn, I was led to a round table with three hosts. Once the cameras were rolling, I was introduced, and one at a time, they each asked. similar questions to what the other interviewers had. After five minutes, I thought their questions were all softballs without any challenge at all. By the time we were done, I realized this was a morning show and was intended to be light entertainment, not hard news.

On my way out, Paula texted me that the CNN remote interview was scheduled for noon. Shortly after that, I received a text from Robert, confirming that both names I sent him were indeed at Orange County Correctional. He asked to be paid by Zelle, which was convenient for me. Although it would leave a money trail that could cost him his job if there were ever an investigation. As for me, I was just paying for information, a normal part of a PI's daily routine.

When I arrived at Seth's office, Paula had a video camera set up in the conference room. The backdrop would be the wall of bookshelves loaded with law books. I'd asked Seth one time if he'd read all those books, and he looked at me like I was crazy, but said he occasionally used them to research prior case law. Alongside the camera were bright lights, aimed to reflect off white umbrellas to prevent glare.

While Paula adjusted the camera, Seth wandered in. "You're doing fantastic on these interviews, Dan. Most people are a nervous wreck, and it comes across on TV. But you always look like a favorite uncle."

"Thanks."

"You'll recall that thirty-day delay we asked for? The judge gave us two days."

"Is that enough?" I asked, concerned.

"Sure. We didn't really need it. We're just trying to drag it out, playing the game. I guess the President has more pull than I do," Seth chortled." It's a preliminary hearing anyway; both sides will present briefs on how they'd like the trial to be conducted. Jury, or no jury. Together or separate. This will be when we find out if they intend to have a military trial for Joe."

"Do I need to prepare?"

"No. I doubt you'll even need to speak. If you do, just be nice to the judge," Seth grinned.

"Of course."

"All right, I'll let you get ready. Good luck."

As noon approached, Paula turned on a monitor so I could see Erin Burnett, the host, who'd be doing the interview. When Erin came on the screen, Paula left the room and closed the door.

While I hadn't met her before, I'd certainly seen Erin many times on television, and she put me at ease right away. "This is all being recorded, so if you make a mistake or need to sneeze, we can just edit it out. Ready?"

"Sure, have at it."

While introducing me, Erin noted for the audience that while our last names were the same, we were unrelated, and after providing some background on the trial, she then began her questions. While she didn't express her own opinions like some of the recent interviewers had, she asked something I wasn't prepared for. When our discussion ventured into the immigrants' legal rights, she asked me to explain them. This was an area where, if I got something even slightly wrong, I'd be crucified. Thinking on my feet, I suggested that an attorney could answer that better than I. We both knew that was a cop-out, but thankfully, she didn't press me on it further. The rest of the interview went well, giving me the room to tell my story.

When I left, there was still time in the day to head back to the office.

"I saw you on CBS this morning," Jim said as I walked in the door.

"How'd I look?"

"Perfect. It seems you guys are winning the war."

"I hope so, but maybe that's because you're not watching Fox News."

Jim laughed. "Maybe I should. Don't they claim to be 'fair and balanced'?"

Then, it was me who laughed, "That was a long time ago."

"When will the trial begin?"

"We have a preliminary hearing next week."

"Are you getting nervous?"

"You mean about spending the rest of my life in prison?"

"That's not really on the table, is it?"

"I have no idea. The charges are serious, and the administration is using this to showcase its will. The only thing that's keeping me calm is having Seth in my corner."

"Yeah, there's that."

We spent the rest of the afternoon reviewing the latest immigrant detention cases that had come in. Jim worked his contact at the Brooklyn Detention Center, and I texted Robert in Orange County. We were able to locate a few of them, but when I asked Robert about one man, he told me that he'd been there for one night, but was shipped out the previous day along with several other immigrants who were picked up at a concrete restoration project in Yonkers. When I asked if he knew where they were taken, he replied, "No."

"Jim, we might have another covert deportation case with Reynaldo Reyes. My guy at Orange County says he was there one night and was shipped out yesterday, along with some others."

"No due process?"

"At least not yet. Although we don't know where they were taken."

"It looks like it's time to earn our keep."

"Yeah, I'll reach out to my contacts in Texas and Florida."

Jim nodded in agreement, while I called Hal Baker and Bobby Lee. After explaining who we were looking for and when they should have arrived, both told me they were on it. While I had confidence in them, I needed to inform Reynaldo's family of what I'd learned. As I glanced through the inquiry information, I steeled myself before making the call.

"Hello, Ms. Reyes?"

"Yes, this is Anna."

"This is Dan Burnett calling about Reynaldo."

"Did you find him?" she asked in excellent English.

As I explained what I'd discovered, she remained silent.

To give her some hope, I said, "But we have some excellent investigators looking for them in places they were likely taken."

She asked, "Where is that?"

"We're looking in Florida and Texas."

"Will you go rescue them like the others?"

Realizing the unrealistic expectations Joe and I had created, I replied, "We don't even know where they are yet, Anna, but a rescue mission is unlikely. I'm already in a world of trouble for the last one."

"Will he be taken to that awful place in El Salvador?"

"I promise we'll work hard to prevent that, but first we need to find them."

Her grief showing through her silence, I offered, "We're doing everything we can, Ma'am. I'll be in touch as soon as we know anything."

After a moment, she replied, "Thank you, Mr. Burnett."

Having overheard the conversation, Jim said, "I assume she didn't take it well?"

"There's really no other way to take it."

"Shall we call it a day, partner?"

"Yeah, I've had enough for today."

**ON MY WAY** to Mia's, I couldn't stop thinking about Anna Reyes. I imagined her visualizing the images shown on TV of all the men bent over with restraints at the prison in El Salvador. All wearing white T-shirts and underwear, while being led like cattle on their way to slaughter. I shivered at the thought of human beings being treated that way. *Were they all violent criminals and gang members deserving of such punishment? If someone like Reynaldo was sent there, what was his crime? Entering a country where he could work hard and raise a family? Was that not the same thing our ancestors did a century or two ago?*

My anger had built as I approached Mamaroneck, but when I pictured sitting with Mia overlooking the Sound, sipping cocktails, it began to ease. When I entered her house and was greeted with a kiss, all was right with the world. At least for the rest of the evening.

# CHAPTER 21

Hal Baker put a call in to his friend at the Department of Corrections and learned that no new groups of immigrants had arrived at any facility in Florida over the last forty-eight hours. He sent Dan a text with that information.

Happy to have work for the day, Bobby Lee got up early and headed to Harlingen, arriving around 11:00 a.m. He had an early lunch at the bar near the airport, where he'd previously seen the workers hanging out after the end of their day. While it wasn't a very appetizing place to eat, he trusted a well-done burger wouldn't kill him. Knowing the airport was open at all hours, he assumed the morning shift would come there as well. They begin to trickle in around noon. Not wanting to approach one of them inside, where everyone would see them talking, Bobby stepped out, hoping to catch someone on their way in.

Standing in the midday sun in southern Texas was no picnic, but he found a shady spot to wait. Within a few minutes, a pickup parked in the lot, and the driver, wearing cowboy boots and a hat, headed for the front door.

"Excuse me. Do you work at the airport?" Bobby asked.

"Yes, I do. My shift is done and I'm ready for a beer."

Bobby handed the man a fifty and said, "Here, buy yourself a few."

The man took the money but looked at Bobby, wondering what this stranger wanted from him.

"Have any ICE flights arrived in the last day or two?" Bobby asked.

"What are you, a reporter?"

"I'm a private investigator," Bobby replied, flashing his license.

After considering whether he should answer, the man said, "Yes. A flight came in yesterday—late morning."

"How many people were aboard?"

"I'm not sure. A half dozen, maybe ten. All beaners in handcuffs."

"Do you know where the flight originated?"

"No, that I wouldn't know."

"Okay, thanks, buddy. If I needed similar information at a later date, how could I get hold of you?"

"You can't." The man gave Bobby a disparaging look and went inside.

Bobby returned to his car, turned the AC to high, and thought to himself, *Shit, it would be nice to get information without driving all the way down here.* He then called Dan Burnett.

"Hey, Dan, It's Bobby."

"What's the good word?"

"There was an ICE flight that landed at Harlingen airport late yesterday morning with six to ten prisoners aboard. I was unable to find out where it originated."

"That fits. What facility would they be taken to?"

"East Hildago Correctional."

"How about you go there and ask to see a prisoner?"

"I can do that. What's the name?"

"Reynaldo Reyes."

"All right, man, talk to you soon."

"Thanks, Bobby. Good work."

**DAN THOUGHT FOR** a moment, wondering if Joe's military contact could confirm where that flight originated. Not quite sure how that relationship worked, he thought he'd leave it to Joe to decide whether he wanted to contact his friend again.

Joe picked up after two rings and announced excitedly, "Hey, Dan. We just got home from the immigration office. Ariana is now a citizen."

"Congratulations, that's awesome."

"Thanks. Somehow, we didn't think she'd need to go through the nightmare that she did."

"I'm sure," I chuckled. "The reason I called is to see if you still have that source for flight plans."

"Sure. What do you need?"

"An ICE flight landed at Harlingen airport yesterday, late morning. I'd love to know where it came from."

"I'll see what I can do."

"Thanks, Joe. Tell Ariana I'm happy for her."

**WHEN BOBBY LEE** walked into the visitors' entrance at the East Hildago Correctional Facility, he went to the main desk and asked to see Reynaldo Reyes.

"Is he a prisoner?"

"Yes."

Balancing reading glasses on the tip of his nose, the man scrolled through his computer screen and said, "There's no one here by that name."

"Is there any name close? Maybe Rays or Ray-es?"

"Nope, sorry."

Once outside the door, Bobby texted Dan, repeating what he'd been told. He then climbed into his car and headed back to Dallas.

**WHILE DAN HAD** been speaking to Bobby, Joe spoke with Major Willis. "Any luck?"

"A flight originating from Stewart Field in Newburgh, New York, arrived at the Harlingen Airport at 10:10 a.m. yesterday."

"Bingo. That confirms our guys are there. Just like Ariana and her friends, they were moved in the middle of the night without any type of hearing whatsoever."

"Cock suckers."

"That's for sure. Thanks, J.T."

**JOE REPORTED HIS** findings to Dan, and after filling in the details, he asked, "Are you ready for court next week?"

"I guess. Seth says not to worry."

"Yeah, Webb says the same thing."

"All right, Joe. Thanks again for the flight information."

Before contacting Mrs. Reyes, Dan called Jim for his thoughts on how to handle it. "I located Reynaldo Reyes in Harlingen, Texas."

"That was quick."

"Yeah, I found a good PI down there. I'm about to notify Mrs. Reyes."

"Good, our work is done. You might as well send her the bill, too."

"I'll do that as soon as I get the PI's bill."

**DAN PUT THE** call in to Anna Reyes.

"Hello."

"Hi, Mrs. Reyes, Dan Burnett calling."

"Yes," she sounded cautious about what he might tell her.

"We located Reynaldo. He's at the East Hidalgo Correctional Facility in Harlingen, Texas." Dan wasn't sure if she would consider this good news or bad news.

"Texas? How did he get there?"

"ICE flew him and some others there so they could avoid an immigration hearing."

"What should I do?"

"I hate to tell you this, Ana, but that's where immigrants are held before they're deported."

Ana burst into tears and cried, "Nooo!"

"I'm sorry, Anna, but listen, they're usually held there for a few days until they have a plane full. Can you afford a lawyer?"

"How much will that cost?"

"A few thousand."

"Maybe. I'll speak with my son," she replied between sobs.

"Okay, while you do that, I'll ask around and see if I can recommend someone. Call me after speaking to your son."

"I will, thank you."

Dan felt terrible for Anna. He'd seen so many people grieve over his years with the NYPD, and knew that many Americans had no understanding of the financial struggles faced by some people, not just immigrants. For families living paycheck to paycheck, an unexpected expense of a few thousand dollars could be overwhelming. And Dan hadn't yet presented Anna with his bill.

He called Justin Miles, the ACLU attorney. "Justin, it's Dan Burnett."

"Hi, Dan. How did Olivia and her mother make out?"

"Everything considered, not too bad. Sophia took your advice and did the self-deportation thing. Olivia will sell her parents' house and send them the money. They're currently living with family in Guatemala."

"Good to hear. What can I do for you?"

"I have another client whose husband was sent to the facility in Harlingen, Texas. I'm hoping you can recommend an attorney for them."

"Oh, man, it's pretty much lawless down there. Let me make some calls and see if I can help. I'll get back to you soon."

"Thanks, Justin. I appreciate it."

Dan realized the day was about over. He'd never left the house, he'd never even had lunch, but a lot had gone down, and his mind was reeling. He wandered into Mia's office and asked, "Did you ever have lunch?"

"I grabbed a yogurt. You were so involved, I didn't want to interrupt."

"That's cool. I'm still expecting a call or two, but then I'll be done for the day."

"Not a problem, love, but it feels like happy hour."

"No kidding."

Dan grabbed a banana to tide him over and made some notes of all the day's events. Then Justin called back.

"Okay, Dan, my counterpart in Corpus Christi is Melissa Bass. She may be able to help your client, and because of the time zones, she'll be in her office for another hour. "

"Great, what's her phone number?"

After Justin relayed the number, he said, "I filled her in on what you told me, but she warned me that things are different there than they are here."

"Yes, I'm well aware. Thanks for this, Justin."

"Happy to help."

Instead of waiting for Anna to call back, Dan called her with the number for the ACLU attorney in Texas.

"Anna?"

"Yes, Dan. I'm still waiting to hear from my son."

"No worries. I found someone in Texas who may be able to help you. She's an attorney with the ACLU."

"Does that mean she works for free?"

"I'm not sure about free, but it will be affordable. She's still in her office if you want to call her."

"I do. What's her number?"

After sharing it, Dan said, "Good luck, Anna. Let me know how it works out."

"Thank you, Dan. Thank you for everything."

After a deep breath, Dan went into the kitchen and shook up a batch of Cosmopolitans. A moment later, Mia joined him. "Cheers!" they exclaimed, taking the first sip before making their way to their happy place.

At the ACLU office in Corpus Christi, the phone rang in the attorney's office.

"Melissa Bass."

"Hello, my name is Anna Reyes. I was given your name by Dan Burnett."

"Yes, Anna. I heard about your husband being moved to East Hildago, and I understand you can't afford an attorney."

"Well, I have some money, but not a few thousand."

"I may be able to help you if you'll make a donation to the ACLU. Whatever you can afford."

"That I can do."

"All right, I'll need to go to the facility and see if they'll confirm that he's there. An attorney has the right to speak to their client in this country, but the detention facilities don't always follow the law down here."

"What do you mean?" Anna asked, not understanding how that could be.

"I'm sorry, but that's just the way it is. What I'll do is go there in the morning and ask to see Reynaldo. Saturdays are big visitation days. If they'll admit that he's there, I'll be able to speak with him and try to arrange a hearing with an immigration judge. But if they don't, there's not much I can do. It would be the same for any attorney, no matter how much they charge."

"Thank you. I think I understand."

"But first, I'll need a signed contract stating that you've hired me to represent you. If I email you a form, can you print it, sign it, and email it back to me?"

"Would I need a scanner?"

"You can just take a picture with your phone and send it to me."

"Okay," Anna said before sharing her email address, knowing her son could help her send a phone picture.

"Good, you'll get the contract in a few minutes. You can send it back anytime tonight, and you'll hear from me by noon, your time, tomorrow."

"Thanks so much, Melissa."

"Let's hope I have good news for you."

REYNALDO REYES WAS woken before sunrise Saturday morning and told to gather his things before being handcuffed. All he had was a prison-issued toothbrush and the clothes he'd come in with. He was then led outside to a waiting bus full of other immigrant detainees. They were taken to an airport and transferred onto an airline jet. After taking off into a rising sun, the plane turned west, and an hour and a half later, they landed in Mexico City. After another bus ride, they were all led into the third prison Reynaldo had been to in four days. This one was the worst by far.

The rank stench of body odor caused Reynaldo to breathe through his mouth. He thought holding his nose would make him look like a sissy, not what you want in jail. The walls had blood spatter, the bedding was ragged, and the toilets and sinks were filthy, with their own nasty smell. This was the first time in his life that Reynaldo thought about killing himself.

MELISSA BASS ENTERED the East Hildago Correctional Facility at 9:00 Saturday morning, hoping to get a head start on all the families who came in for their weekly visitations. She strode confidently to the desk with her attorney-client contract and announced she was there to see a prisoner by the name of Reynaldo Reyes. She was quickly told there was no one there by that name. Melissa's heart sank, and she wanted to scream. She wanted to dive over the counter and look at the screen herself. "Look, I know he's here. He came with a group from New York two days ago."

"I'm sorry, ma'am. All I know is what's on my screen."

Defeated, she walked out to her car, dreading the call she was about to make. For the third time that week, she thought about asking for a transfer out of Texas. *Fucking Texas!*

DAN AND MIA spent the weekend on *Privateer*. They sailed to their favorite quiet cove near Greenwich, Connecticut. Anchored securely, they enjoyed a peaceful evening, eating grilled lamb chops, sipping a good bottle of Montepulciano, and making love under the stars.

THIRTY-SIX-YEAR-OLD JOSH VOLPE was laying out his clothes for his appearance in court the following day. After finishing law school, he'd made his way up through the ranks and, for the last few years, had been working as a Federal Prosecutor for the Southern District of New York. He'd gained a good reputation in the district for prosecuting immigrants.

Tomorrow would be the day he'd been waiting for, the reason he'd gone to law school, and become a prosecutor. Ever since 9/11, when he was just twelve years old, he'd been seeking revenge for the death of his parents at the World Trade Center. Tomorrow, he would finally get his chance.

# CHAPTER 22

I awoke Monday morning with the day's court appearance on my mind. This was the first day of a trial that I feared would be long and tedious.

Having put on a dress shirt and slacks, I fretted over wearing a tie. After putting one on and taking it off, I chose to wear just a tweed sport coat. Mia sat with me while I ate breakfast, my usual fruit and yogurt, then wished me luck with a kiss on the way out the door. Unlike most people, I'd testified in court many times as a cop and knew what to expect, yet I was still apprehensive.

The hearing would be held at the federal district court, just two blocks from Seth's office in White Plains. The front steps were lined with media, including their microphones, recorders, and camera crews. A few protestors held signs that read, "Muslims Have Rights Too", "Due Process for All", and others supporting our side.

When the reporters saw me approach the steps, I was mobbed with microphones stuck in my face as they shouted questions at me. Per Seth's instructions, I said, "No comment," multiple times.

Elsa was waiting for me at the top and asked, "How are you feeling?"

"I feel good." I suspected that sound bite would make it to the evening news.

Once inside the building, I saw Joe waiting on a bench just outside the locked courtroom. We sat and made small talk. The hour before the doors opened was when lawyers met with prosecutors and cut plea deals if the cases were nearing conclusion.

Joe was dressed like I was, not in uniform, since one of the charges was impersonating an officer. We saw Seth and Webb come around the corner where the judges' chambers were, and assumed they'd been filing last-minute briefs.

"Good morning, gentlemen," Seth greeted. "We're up first today."

When the courtroom doors opened, we followed *our* attorneys in toward a table beyond the rail on the left side. Seth and Web, who sat together between Joe and me, took some files out of their briefcases before stashing them below the table. When the prosecutors arrived, they approached our table and introduced themselves as if they were old friends. I recognized Josh Volpe from the day workers' trial with Hector Martinez. The two others, Gloria Levine and Randall Smith, were unfamiliar.

The gallery was allowed to enter, and the courtroom was soon filled to capacity. We heard, "All rise," as Judge Ferris took his seat in the front of the courtroom at an elevated dark wood desk that appeared to have been there for decades. The entire courtroom was paneled in a rich, matching wood.

The judge announced, "I'd like to start today by acknowledging the immense public interest in this trial, thus the full courtroom. Under these circumstances, I will allow no sound whatsoever from the gallery and will instruct the bailiff to remove anyone from this courtroom who violates that order."

He continued, "All right, I've reviewed the briefs from counsel, of which there are many. Today, we will decide the framework for this trial, whether the defendants will be tried together or separately, and whether it will be a trial by jury or by the powers granted to me. Mr. Volpe, you may proceed."

Josh Volpe stood and said, "Thank you, Your Honor. As you saw from our briefs, we move that the defendants be tried individually due to the difference in charges. Some of Mr. Wilkinson's charges stem from military violations that have nothing to do with the charges levied against Mr. Burnett."

"Mr. Bodner, I see you've elected to be the lead defense counsel. How do you respond to the prosecution's motion?"

Seth stood. "Your Honor, only one of the charges is different for Mr. Wilkinson. If counsel felt that his charges required special treatment, they could have moved for a military trial. And, as you saw from our motion, it is not unlawful for military personnel to wear their uniform after retirement. We request that the charge of impersonating an officer be dismissed."

"Noted, Mr. Bodner. Mr. Volpe provided me with a written response to your motion just this morning. I've yet to digest it thoroughly."

"Thank you, Your Honor. Additionally, to save the court's time and expense, the defense moves that the defendants be tried together. Mr. Burnett will be happy to sit through any proceeding that only applies to Mr. Wilkinson."

"Thank you, counselor," Judge Ferris responded. "Mr. Volpe, what is your position on a jury trial?"

"Your Honor, to the point Mr. Bodner raised about saving time and expense, we move for a bench trial. With all the media attention around this trial, we believe it will be difficult to select an unbiased jury."

"Mr. Bodner, your response?"

"Your Honor, as we presented in our brief, a case of this magnitude all but requires a jury trial. The verdict must reflect the values and standards of the general public. Additionally, with the deeply divided political environment we find ourselves in, a jury trial will protect this court from accusations of bias."

"Mr. Volpe, I'll grant you a brief response."

"Your Honor, the defense is clearly hoping to reap the rewards of the public relations campaign they've been waging. We stand by our belief that an unbiased jury will be difficult to seat."

"Thank you, counselors. We'll take a fifteen-minute break before I rule on these matters."

"All rise," the bailiff announced as Judge Ferris left the bench.

While standing, everyone in the courtroom noted the time before filing out.

When Dan and Joe huddled with their attorneys in the hall, Webb spoke in a hushed tone, "That was interesting."

Dan and Joe wondered what he was referring to.

Seth smiled. "I think you scared them off a court-martial, Webb."

"Perhaps."

"Any guess on how he'll rule?" Joe asked.

"The judge would be a fool to take the responsibility of this verdict on by himself. He'll be crucified by the losing side, whoever that is," Webb offered.

Seth nodded in agreement before saying, "Okay. Let's all go take a leak and get a sip of water."

When the court resumed, Judge Ferris said, "Thank you, counselors, for your well-prepared arguments. Regarding separate hearings, I believe counsel had the opportunity to try Mr. Wilkinson in a military courtroom if they believed his case was so unique. Therefore, we will try both men together.

"Regarding the charge of impersonating an officer, the court will dismiss that charge against Mr. Wilkinson. As for a jury or bench trial, in a case with this much national attention, the defendants deserve a judgment by their peers. We will meet the potential jurors in three days, on Thursday at 10:00 a.m." With a stroke of his gavel, the court was adjourned.

Once the judge exited, the attorneys on both sides muttered in disbelief.

Astonished, Webb said, "Three days?"

"Let's have lunch in my office," Seth said. "We have a lot of work to do."

"That's an understatement," Webb agreed.

On the way over, we had purpose in our step. We'd gotten everything we asked for, and the quick jury selection phase would be just as challenging for the prosecution as it would be for us. When we walked into the office, Paula read each of our faces, trying to determine the outcome.

She said, "Judging from your body language, I assume it went well?"

We all nodded.

Seth said," We meet the jurors in three days."

"Oh, my. Shall I cancel your appointments?"

"Anything that isn't pressing."

"Got it. I assume you'd like sandwiches?"

"Please. Thanks, Paula."

When we were seated in the conference room, Seth said, "First thing we need is a jury consultant. Webb, what do you think of Joyce Waters?"

"She's great if she's available," Webb replied

"I'll call her right now before the prosecution snags her."

We heard Seth's side of the phone conversation and became concerned when he said, "That's right, three days—Thursday." Our concern eased when he added, "Great, we'll see you in the morning." After Seth hung up, he asked, "How's your schedule look, Dan?"

"Nothing more important than this."

"Good. As soon as we get the list of jurors, we need to begin investigating them. It will save us some money if you can do it. Can Jim help you? There will be at least twenty names, maybe thirty," Seth added.

"I'll ask."

"He's got to give us until Monday for selection, don't you think?" Webb questioned.

"I hope so. This case has garnered significant national interest, particularly for the President."

Joe and I felt out of place, watching our attorneys make to-do lists and scramble to prepare. Soon, Paula carried in a tray of sandwiches and Diet Cokes, along with glasses filled with ice. "What can I do?" she asked.

Webb and Seth looked at each other before Seth said, "Start looking into case law for interfering with a government proceeding. If there's anything regarding interfering with deportations, focus on that as well."

Webb nodded, "Yes, that's where we're most vulnerable."

Joe and I didn't have much to do, other than eat. When I was done, I sent a text to Jim, asking for some of his time on Friday or Saturday. While I was doing that, Joe asked how he could help.

"Get with Paula and see if she can set up any more appearances for you over the weekend," Seth suggested.

As Joe rose, I asked, "Do you need anything more from us today?"

Seth said, "I guess not. On Thursday, we'll meet the jurors for the first time. Their first reaction to you and Joe will be telling. They'll also hear about the case and the charges for the first time. What do you think, Webb, should Joe be in uniform?"

Webb sat back in his chair, thinking. "Let's let our jury consultant make that call."

"All right. See you guys tomorrow," I said as Joe and I walked out of the conference room. I waited for him to discuss media appearances with Paula so we could walk out together.

While riding down the elevator, Joe said, "I had no idea of the psychology involved with picking a jury."

"I've heard it said that cases are won or lost on jury selection day," I chortled.

We bumped fists before going our separate ways.

**WHEN I ARRIVED** a Mia's, it was only mid-afternoon, but she was already in her loungewear. This time, it was a velour outfit with an oversized, off-the-shoulder boat-neck top and fitted pants. She greeted me with a smile and a kiss, and I could tell she'd just bathed. When I nuzzled her neck, I caught a hint of her scent, and whatever tension I'd been carrying vanished. After hugging, I stepped back to arm's length and looked at her, admiring her comfortable beauty and the perfection of her smiling face.

"I know it's a little early, but how about making us a martini, love?" she said softly, moving closer with her head on my chest.

"I can't say no to that," I replied, gently tipping her chin up to meet my lips.

After making the drinks, we settled into our happy place with Mia snuggled into my shoulder. "So tell me about your day," she inquired. I shared all the details, and she commented, "That sounds pretty positive to me."

"It is, other than the push to select a jury. Seth wants me to investigate each of the potential jurors. I'm hoping Jim can help."

Most afternoons, we'd be focused on the activity in the Sound, but that day, Mia occupied all my senses, and it wasn't long before we ended up in bed.

Once we'd recovered, Mia slipped the velour outfit back on and went down to prepare dinner, while I checked messages. Jim told me he was open all day Saturday, and Seth wanted me to come in to meet the jury specialist in the morning.

I joined Mia in the kitchen, put my arms around her from behind, and said, "Thank you, sweetheart, that was just what I needed."

She turned her head back, gave me a quick kiss on the lips, and smiled, "You might recall that I enjoyed it, too."

After opening a bottle of white wine, I poured each of us a glass and sat at the counter, watching her cook. She had the TV on in the sitting area behind me, with the volume low. When the local news came on, the lead story was about our hearing that day, with the image of the court steps filled with reporters and protesters. I turned up the volume, not to learn anything new, but to gauge the public's reaction. While it seemed that we had them on our side, I knew I was only witnessing the people who came out to support us. There was a slice of the public who did not, and other media outlets that were working against us.

We sat down to a dinner of baked trout with a pecan and dill top crust, along with wild rice. I again tried to imagine what I ever did to deserve a woman like Mia.


JOYCE WATERS, THE jury consultant, seemed to know all about our case. I assumed Seth had briefed her, but she was also well-versed in the public opinion surrounding our case.

When the three of us sat down in the conference room, she said, "I've been following your achievements for the last year or two, Dan. You've somehow been able to solve the most prominent cases—I'm impressed."

"Thanks. Give credit to the City of New York for thirty years of training."

"That's very modest; I'm sure it's more than that," she replied, looking me square in the eye. She made a professional appearance, wearing a skirt and blouse that were attractive yet business-like. With dark hair and stylish glasses, I guessed her age at fortyish.

"All right, Joyce. What are we dealing with here?" Seth asked.

"Well, we have multiple factors. First, the Muslim thing, then we have immigration, the military, and the political environment. We'll want to avoid Republicans, Fox News watchers, and anyone who was involved, or lost loved ones on 9/11. Those are the easy ones."

"So that's what we need to screen for?" I asked.

"Again, those are the easy ones. I'll look for other traits during the interview process."

"How about authority figures?" Seth asked.

"That can go two ways; there is the current government authority, as opposed to military authority. Some people view anyone in uniform as the police."

"So, you're suggesting that Colonel Wilkinson attend the hearings in plain clothes?"

"That's my first inclination. But let's see who we actually seat."

"Besides social media and public records, what other information sources should I be looking at?" I asked.

"It's very hard to determine what people watch on TV. We have no way to access their viewing habits, and Nielsen ratings are only in the aggregate; you can't track individuals. Believe it or not, observing their homes and cars is often a good way to determine political views."

"Yup," I agreed.

"Bumper stickers and NRA logos near their front doors. Things like that. And, of course, social media."

I nodded, understanding. Most of this I knew from my years on the force, and over the last few years, social media had become the first place to look. I'm amazed by what can be learned online.

"After meeting the jury pool on Thursday, I'll prepare a list of questions about each individual," Joyce said.

"Do you have any other questions, Dan?" Seth asked.

"No, I think I'm good. If you have nothing else, I'll see you tomorrow."

"Nope, that's it."

"Nice to finally meet you," Joyce said.

"Likewise."

I spent the rest of the day at the Marina hoping to unwind. But while washing Privateer, I found myself imagining scenes in the courtroom. While I'd been unable to clear my head, at least the boat was clean.

# CHAPTER 23

With almost fifty potential jurors in the pool, our first contact with them was in an assembly room just inside the entrance to the courthouse. There were a couple of tables in front for the opposing counsels, one on each side of the judges' elevated lectern. The potential jurors who'd been called in to serve were already seated, some chatting, some scrolling through their phones, as Joe and I entered along with our attorneys.

Joe was dressed in a sport coat and slacks with no tie, as was I. Our attorneys wore suits and ties, with Joyce in a skirt suit. Once seated, she leaned over the table enough to make eye contact, first with me, and then with Joe. "The jurors will be getting their first impressions of you. It's essential that you appear comfortable and relaxed, and don't avoid eye contact. Take note of anyone who looks at you with hatred."

After acknowledging the opposition, the bailiff asked us to rise as Judge Ferris entered the assembly room.

"Good morning, everyone. Good morning, counselors."

Everyone nodded.

The judge continued, "Due to the national exposure this case has received, and the size of the jury pool, I'm going to extend the jury selection to a few days. While this is somewhat unusual, in this case, I feel it necessary to allow counsel additional time for research."

Before me, I saw a diverse group of people of all ages, races, and walks of life. For the most part, they looked at us from the tables with curiosity, and I saw no distinct hatred in anyone's eyes.

The judge proceeded to thank them all for taking time out of their busy schedules to perform a duty that is crucial to our system of justice. He spoke for another five minutes on that subject before explaining the charges that Joe and I faced. Because we'd been all over the news for the past month, they seemed to be familiar with the case. The judge explained how the jury selection process would proceed and asked if any of them personally knew anyone sitting at the tables.

With no indication of a yes, he asked if anyone had difficulty understanding the English language. It seemed that about a third of them raised their hands. After thanking them for appearing, he dismissed them. Next, he informed the remaining pool that he expected the trial to last for a week or more, and asked if serving would be an undue hardship for anyone.

One gentleman raised his hand and explained that his wife was in the hospital, and he needed to be home to care for their children. The judge thanked him for fulfilling his duty and excused him. He walked out relieved. Two others claimed they could not be away from work for that long, and the judge also excused them. By my count, there were twenty-four remaining.

The bailiff then assigned each of them a juror number, and Judge Ferris announced that we'd all move to the courtroom to begin the interview process, known as "voir dire".

It took several minutes to reassemble in the courtroom, with us sitting at the tables as we had before, Joe and I on the outside and Joyce in the middle. The jury box was large enough to seat the now-reduced number of jurors. Within a few minutes, the bailiff delivered the jurors' questionnaires and numbers to the attorneys.

After going through the "all rise" process again, Judge Ferris took his seat at the bench, welcomed everyone, and then asked Juror Number One to stand and state his name. An older white gentleman rose, introduced himself, and then took his seat again. The judge said, "Mr. Bodner, you may begin."

Seth nodded, rose, and approached the jury box in a friendly, unthreatening manner, keeping a respectful distance. To lighten the moment, Seth performed a shtick about how young he looked. He got a smile not only from Juror Number One, but from the whole pool. Once he'd convinced them he was old enough to be there, he asked Juror Number One if he was familiar with the case.

At first, a bit nervous, he answered, "Yes. I've seen it on TV."

"Have you seen either of the defendants on television?"

"Yes, I saw the Colonel on *60 Minutes* with his wife."

Having the juror acknowledge that he knew Joe was a colonel would be telling to the attorneys, and I noticed Joyce taking notes on her laptop.

"Based on that television appearance, have you formed an opinion of Mr. Wilkinson?" Seth asked.

"I'd say he's an honest man who loves his wife."

"Is that the only time you've seen him?"

"Yes."

"Have you seen or read about the events of this case anywhere other than *60 Minutes*?"

"Sure, who hasn't?"

His response drew a chuckle from most of those in attendance.

"This will be my last question, sir. Do you believe you can make a fair and open-minded judgment of the defendants, based solely on the evidence heard in this courtroom?"

"Yes, sir," Juror Number One replied.

"Thank you," Seth said before returning to the table.

Judge Ferris said, "Mr. Volpe, you may approach the jury box."

As Josh Volpe rose, he said, "Thank you, Your Honor."

Without any rehearsed opening, he walked toward the jurors, keeping the same distance as Seth. "Good morning," he greeted Juror Number One.

"Good morning," the older gentleman replied.

"Did you serve in the military, Sir?"

"Yes, sir. I was a second lieutenant in the Navy from 1971 to 1975."

"So that was during the Vietnam War?"

"Toward the end of it."

"Do you have an opinion of that war?"

"My opinion has changed over the years. When I served, I believed in the effort a hundred percent, but since then I've come to believe it was all a mistake."

"I see. Where were you during 9/11?"

"Right here in White Plains, I've lived here all my life."

"How do you feel about that attack on our nation?"

"I was horrified. Like everyone, I never thought our country could be attacked like that. To watch the planes fly into those buildings was like watching special effects in a movie."

"Do you hold any ill will for the people who committed the attacks?"

"Well, they all died during the attack, and as for Bin Laden, we got him too."

"Do you have an opinion of the Muslim people in general?"

"It's just a religion. I'm sure they grew up believing in it because their parents did. Just like Catholics here, it's what they believe."

"Thank you. That's all I have for now," Josh said.

Judge Ferris said, "Thank you."

As the prosecutor returned to his seat, I noticed Joyce had drawn a star on the list next to Juror Number One.

Judge Ferris gestured for the next juror to rise. Juror Number Two was a white woman in her late forties who initially appeared to be a housewife. I imagined her kids were in high school.

The judge said, "Mr. Volpe."

"Thank you, Your Honor. Good morning, ma'am."

"Good morning."

"Is there any reason that you cannot be a fair and impartial juror in the case before us today?"

"No."

"The form you filled out says you're a teacher in Larchmont. What do you teach?"

"Eighth-grade science."

"Have you seen any of the publicity around this case?"

"Yes, on the news most nights."

"Can you recall any specific segment involving the case?"

"I do. I've seen Elsa Nordstrom interview Mr. Burnett."

"How many times have you seen him on TV?"

She thought for a moment before replying. "Once about this case, and also when Elsa interviewed him last year after he captured the 'nurse murderer.'"

"That's all I have today, thank you, ma'am."

"Mr. Bodner," the judge said, "do you have any questions for this juror?"

By the way he addressed Seth, I thought the judge figured Juror Number Two was a no-brainer for the defense, but I also thought Seth would show her respect by not declining to question her. I was right.

"Yes, Your Honor," he said as he stood. "Do you consider yourself a religious person?"

"Not really. I was raised as a Protestant and was married in a Protestant church, but to be honest, I haven't been back since."

"How did you feel about the attack on 9/11?"

"I hate those people."

"When you say 'those people', are you referring to the Muslim religion?"

Without pause, she answered, "No, just the ones who carried out the attack."

"Thank you, ma'am. That's all I have."

I noticed that Joyce put a question mark alongside her number.

This went on until 12:30, at which point the judge called for a lunch break. We'd made it through nine of the potential twenty-four jurors.

At the luncheonette across the street, Joe, me, and the defense team took a booth for four, and I pulled up a chair at the end. While I'd found the questioning to be somewhat interesting, Joyce and the two attorneys were pumped. They asked one another what they thought about each juror's response to almost every question, gauging how they would view the case. While most of the jurors' answers seemed pretty much down the middle to me, they were discussing body language and the tells of lying. Joe and I remained silent and listened to them work.

As many times as I had testified in court over the years, I'd never been part of jury selection. Seth, Webb, and Joyce were talking about peremptory challenges and challenges for cause. And about which challenges would be used for which juror. While they had mixed feelings on most of them, Juror Number One stood out as the most likely to side with the defense. For that reason, they assumed the prosecution would challenge him.

Once we'd returned to the courtroom, the questioning resumed, with each side rotating who would go first. One change was that Webb would conduct the interviews for our side. Right away, I noticed that his tone was more fatherly than Seth's. He came across as an elder statesman, yet he was younger than I.

It wasn't difficult to understand what each side was looking for, and by that time, the jury pool understood as well—you could hear it in their answers. After making it through the next six jurors in what had become a routine manner, Juror Number Seventeen threw us a curve. She was a Black woman in her early thirties from Elmsford, dressed in casual clothing, and it soon appeared that Josh Volpe had not read the jury questionnaire. Assuming she was uneducated, he asked about her children, her religion, and her husband. When she told him she was divorced, I thought Josh already had her pegged as someone who'd just go along with the consensus when it came time for a verdict.

When it was Webb's turn, the first question he asked was where she worked. "I'm a pharmacist at Memorial Sloan Kettering," was her answer, catching many by surprise.

"Where did you go to school?"

"I received my doctorate at Columbia."

I sensed Webb felt like he'd opened a door, while the prosecutor rummaged through the questionnaires.

"How long did that take you?" Webb asked.

"Six years, seven counting my residency."

"Just about everyone has been asked about 9/11 today, so I'll ask you. Do you remember where you were that day?"

"I'd just started my freshman year at Columbia. They cancelled classes, and we gathered in the social room at our dorm and watched it on TV. I remember calling my parents that morning. Everyone was crying and in disbelief."

"Did you hate the men who flew the planes?"

"Of course! But not because they were Muslims. I was dating my former husband at the time, and he's a Muslim. He was more upset than anyone else. I know the Muslim people are peaceful."

"Thank you, ma'am. I hope I didn't upset you," Webb said in his fatherly tone.

The prosecution table was in shock. Webb had managed to make a major case point that all the jurors witnessed, and the trial had not yet begun.

Joyce put a star next to Juror Number Seventeen.

**WE DID MANAGE** to get through all the prospective jurors that day. Judge Ferris thanked them for participating in the justice system before asking the counselors if they'd like the weekend to prepare for the final jury selection. Both tables answered with a resounding, "Yes, Your Honor."

"All right, this hearing is in recess until 10:00 Monday morning."

It was 5:30 when we exited the courtroom. Joyce told me she'd email her list of interests to me that evening, and Seth said he'd be available anytime. We all shook hands and went our separate ways. I'd already texted Mia that I'd be late.

It was 7:00 by the time we had our cocktail, this time, a Martini.

"Since I knew you'd be late, I thawed some Bolognese sauce for tonight. I hope that's okay." Mia looked up at me with her sparkling eyes, reflecting the setting sunlight through the glass.

I kissed her forehead and replied, "Of course. I love your spaghetti."

"So tell me about your day in court."

I went through the day, in as much detail as I thought she'd want to hear, but went a little deeper on Juror Seventeen. Mia was fascinated by the turn in that interview and immediately caught its significance. I told her about the judge granting us the weekend to prepare and that I'd be busy researching the jurors' backgrounds for the next few days.

**I AWOKE ON** Thursday, remembering that Joyce said she'd send me her list of jury pool questions. When I found her email, I noticed that some questions applied to everyone, while others were tailored to a particular juror. It didn't take long to realize I'd need to put this into spreadsheet form to keep track of it all.

With a cup of coffee by my side, I sat at the dining room table and went to work. After coming up with a column layout, it took me about an hour to create the spreadsheet. By then, Mia was up, and she brought me a bowl of fruit before heading into the city for the day.

I considered going to the office, but decided I could handle all the online work from home. I began with voter registration records and found that each town was different. Soon enough, I had everyone's party affiliation listed. Next up were the property tax records, and again, each town was unique. From those, I could determine if they owned a house or a car, and what the value was. I could also check if they were in arrears on their taxes.

As for whether they had children, that information was on the juror questionnaire, along with their marital status, age, occupation, and education level. With that knowledge, I conducted a Google search for each name, finding at least some information for each of them. There were links to social media, business affiliations, group memberships, and other relevant connections. A few of them had written letters to the editor of one newspaper or another, with a link to their letter appearing in the search. One thing that slowed me down was if they had a common name, and there were multiple hits. Then I'd have to dig deeper to see which one I was looking at. The Google search took me till noon.

After eating a sandwich, I began digging into social media—this went slower. If I found them listed, I'd view their profiles, which, in most cases, if they had their privacy settings set to public, allowed me to see every post, providing a great indication of their interests and political leanings. I had a column devoted to politics. One could quickly see how deeply divided this country was, from posts that had been liked or shared.

By the time I got through all the social media sites, it was nearing the end of the day. I sat back and reviewed all the information I'd collected, happy that I'd created the spreadsheet. I could immediately identify where there were holes. If someone did not own a home, was not registered to vote, or had no social media presence, a blank box would appear.

When I saw Mia pull into the driveway, I sent what I had off to Joyce, noting that I'd fill in the blanks tomorrow.

The following morning, I drove to the office, and for once I actually arrived before Jim. Shortly after I started the coffee pot, he came through the door, surprised to see me. "What brings you in so early?"

"I don't know, I guess I'm feeling the pressure to complete the juror research."

Once we each had a coffee, I shared my spreadsheet with him. After a moment, he said, "Wow. It looks like you're almost done."

"That's all the stuff off the internet. The blank boxes will require some shoe leather."

While digesting the spreadsheet, Jim tipped his head to the side and cracked his neck, something I hadn't seen him do in a while.

It was a habit of his when he was thinking. He said, "So what do we do, drive by the houses looking for bumper stickers on the cars?"

"Yeah, you know the drill. I was thinking we'd split them up by towns, north and south."

It didn't take long to divide them. Jim chose the southern coastal towns, while I took the northern part of the county. On our way out, I asked if there were any new inquiries about detained immigrants.

"We're still getting calls, but not like before. I don't know if that's because of fewer ICE raids locally, or that you haven't been on TV lately."

I shrugged. "Did you hear about ICE questioning kids playing baseball in Harlem?"

"No. You'd think children would be off limits," Jim replied.

"It appears there *are* no limits."


I STARTED WITH the northernmost town on my list, which was Katonah. The house was large and valuable, which surprised me because the tax records didn't list the juror's name as the owner. That indicated they were renters, either transient or having weak credit, too weak for a mortgage. The driveway was gated, and the house sat back from the road, so there was no way to see bumper stickers. The only note I could add to the spreadsheet was that the address listed for the juror was an expensive *rented* home. And without a license plate number, I couldn't find out where their car was registered. That was a strikeout.

The next address was in Bedford Hills, again a wealthy town. While this was a grand, older home, the number of cars in the driveway indicated it was also a rental, but rented by multiple people. Looking at the information on the spreadsheet, I noted that the juror's age was twenty-four and assumed they rented a room or lived with friends or family. The car was registered here, so I knew the make and saw it in the driveway with no bumper stickers. I made notes on the spreadsheet and moved on to Mount Kisco.

At the first address, I found a modest colonial home in a neighborhood of similar houses. There were no cars in the driveway, and from the road, I saw nothing that would identify a religious or political association.

At the second house in Mount Kisco, I found some more telling information. Two vehicles were in the driveway: a car and a pickup, both with Trump bumper stickers. The truck also had an NRA sticker on the back window, and a boat and trailer were parked alongside the garage.

By mid-afternoon, I'd driven by a dozen addresses in northern Westchester County, with varying results, and made handwritten notes for each one on the spreadsheet. While there were still a few blank boxes, I texted Jim that I was done and fairly close to the office. He replied that he was on his way back.

Once there, we compared notes, and I entered the information into the computer, creating a clean copy to email to Joyce and both attorneys. Jim and I then went next door to the Outback for a burger and a beer on me.

# CHAPTER 24

Seth, Webb, and Joyce gathered in Seth's office on Sunday morning. The mission for the day was to formulate a strategic plan to use their challenges. Now that they had the investigation summary from Dan, they could decide who they wanted on the jury and who they didn't. They also knew the prosecution would be doing the same.

From the investigation summary and the courtroom questioning, they worked their way through the list, marking a "yes" or "no" next to each juror's number. If they were a strong yes or no, Joyce would mark that accordingly. For the criteria, they thought that Democrats, minorities, religious people, and those with children would most likely be empathetic to the Muslim immigrants, while the opposite would be more likely to side with the prosecution. Additionally, they believed someone who lost loved ones on 9/11 would favor the prosecution.

While they knew that wouldn't always hold true, they were dealing with likelihoods. They knew they'd be calling a constitutional law professor to testify and wanted jurors who would understand that testimony. Their overriding goal was to focus the trial on following constitutional law and demonstrating how the Justice Department and ICE had violated it by usurping due process. They also knew the prosecution would steer the trial toward the defendants' interference with government agencies and the hijacking of a government plane. To combat the latter charge, Webb planned to bring in a hijacking expert he knew from the National Transportation Safety Board.

Once they'd prepared their list of yes's and no's, along with the toss-ups, they moved on to the challenge strategy.

Their strongest yeses were numbers 1, 6, and 17. The strongest no's were numbers 8, 16, and 22. Their strategic goal was to have the prosecution exhaust their six peremptory challenges before reaching number 17, and to reserve one of their remaining challenges to use for number 22.

As for challenges for cause, these would arise in cases where the juror was unusually familiar with the case, had a previous acquaintance with a defendant, attorney, or witness, or, for some reason, was unable to judge the case fairly due to prejudice or religious beliefs. There was no limit on challenges for cause, but they would be granted at the judge's discretion.

They spent the next hour doing a mock selection by the numbers and were certain the prosecution would use a peremptory challenge for juror number one. The next few were toss-ups in their minds, but they planned to use a peremptory challenge for numbers 8, 16, and 22 due to political affiliation, with number 16 also having lost a brother during 9/11. While the actual process would be fluid, they ran through a few mock scenarios in preparation.

Once they had a feel for who the jury would be, few had shown any favorable opinion of the military, so they decided that Joe should attend the trial in street clothes and that Ariana's presence as the loving wife would be a positive influence. With that accomplished, they all went home to get some rest before the long, grueling days ahead.

ON MONDAY MORNING, Dan and Joe made their way up the courthouse steps, surrounded by a mob of reporters. Even Elsa Nordstrom received a "no comment" to her shouted questions.

Once inside the lobby, they huddled with their attorneys for last-minute instructions. Again, Joyce asked to be informed if either of them received any hateful looks from the jury pool. After taking their seats in the courtroom, the bailiff and Judge Ferris went through their ritual, and the final jury selection began.

First up was Juror Number One, who, as expected, was dismissed with a peremptory challenge by Josh Volpe. He hadn't asked even one question.

Next was Juror Number Two. Continuing with the alternating order, Seth approached the jury box and asked if they knew anyone who was killed on 9/11. Receiving an answer of no, he asked if they had a predetermined opinion of the case. With another no, Seth told the judge that he would welcome them to the jury. Josh stood briefly and said that he, too, would accept this juror.

When Juror Number Three's turn came, Josh approached and asked if she had any Muslim friends. After she answered yes, Josh asked her to describe the nature of their relationship.

"Well, the family who lives next door to us is Muslim, and our children play together almost every day."

"Based on your interactions with them, have you formed an opinion about their religion?"

"They seem quite ordinary to me. Actually, I've never really considered them as different in any way."

"Has your relationship with your neighbors caused you to form a preconceived notion of the facts in this case?"

"I have no idea what the facts of this case are," she answered, with a hint of humor showing through.

"So, you're telling me that you'll be able to judge this case fairly, based solely on the evidence presented during this trial?"

"Yes," she replied.

"Thank you, ma'am. That's all I have."

"Mr. Bodner, your turn," the judge said.

"Thank you, Your Honor. We welcome this juror to the trial."

"Mr. Volpe?"

"Your Honor, we challenge this juror for cause."

Everyone at the defense table looked up for Judge Ferris's response.

"And what would the cause be, Mr. Volpe?" he asked.

"Her admitted relationship with a Muslim family."

"Denied, Mr. Volpe."

"We'll then use a peremptory challenge, Your Honor."

"Very well. Juror Number Three, you are excused."

The defense table silently celebrated that the prosecution had burned two of their peremptory challenges among the first three jurors.

As the questioning of jurors continued, the prosecution used another peremptory challenge for Juror Number Six, leaving them with three remaining.

The defense used its first challenge on Juror Number Eight.

When it was Seth's next turn with a witness, his questions began to search for information that would be unfavorable to the prosecution, hoping they would exhaust their challenges before reaching Juror Number Seventeen.

Without any success through the next few, when he inquired about political affiliation with Number Eleven, the response was, "Oh yes, I've been involved with the Democratic party most of my life. In fact, I organized the biggest fundraiser in the history of Westchester County for Barack Obama."

"Thank you, sir," Seth said. "That's all I have, Your Honor."

Josh Volpe used another peremptory challenge with Juror Eleven, without asking a question.

While Josh Volpe was interviewing Juror Twelve, the defense table huddled again, calculating how to influence the prosecution to use their remaining peremptory challenges before they reached Juror Seventeen.

The prosecution used one more on Juror Fourteen, a man who'd been in and out of jail a few times for misdemeanor charges. If they had been felony charges, he would have never received a notice to serve on a jury.

It was then time for the lunch break, and everyone filed out of the courtroom, with the prosecution having only one challenge remaining.

While at lunch, at the same luncheonette across the street where they'd gone before, the attorneys reviewed how they'd fared so far. While they felt good about preventing Number Eight from serving, and still having almost all of their challenges remaining, they felt certain the prosecution would use their last on Number Seventeen, the Black female pharmacist, who'd rocked the prosecution during the initial interviews. Joyce scanned through the remaining jurors and saw one other who might be unfavorable to the prosecution. Juror Number Twenty, a Methodist minister. She wishfully hoped the prosecution was saving its last challenge for him.

When the court reconvened, Seth began his questioning of Juror Fifteen by asking if he knew anyone who was killed at the World Trade Center. The answer was no. His questions then shifted to topics he hoped would bait the prosecution into using their last challenge. He inquired about religious and political affiliations and asked if he had formed an opinion after seeing the defendants on television. All of his answers were neutral and credible. When it was the prosecution's turn, after just a few questions, Josh Volpe announced that he would accept this juror. The defense agreed.

Seth used another challenge for Juror Number sixteen, the juror that Dan had discovered with the bumper stickers on his vehicles.

Next up was the pharmacist, Number Seventeen. Without asking a single question, the prosecution used its final peremptory challenge.

By the time they'd finished with Juror Number Twenty, the required twelve had been seated, although the process continued to select two alternates out of the four remaining candidates. Seth used a peremptory challenge for Number Twenty-Two, and after just a few questions, he accepted Number Twenty-Three, completing the jury selection process.

Judge Ferris thanked the jurors for their service and thanked the counselors for the professional process. He then announced, "The court is in recess until tomorrow at 10:00 a.m."

Before rising from the table, Joyce said, "Nice job, gentleman. While we didn't get everyone we wanted, we can win with this jury."

Webb nodded. "I think so, too."

"I'm going back to the office to prepare some briefs with Paula. She found some case law that should be helpful," Seth said. "Good night, everyone."

While walking, Seth relived every moment of the day, what he could have done differently, and how he could have planned better. He really wanted Juror Seventeen; she had the character to lead the deliberations. *Shit. We came so close.*

While driving, Dan thought about the performance of their attorneys, the way they planned, and how they switched gears when necessary. He was especially impressed by the way Seth kept his cool all day.

When Dan arrived at Mia's, she was welcoming as always. With a kiss and a cocktail ready, she wanted to hear how the jury selection went. Dan replayed the day, telling her about their success in eliminating the jurors they were concerned about, as well as the disappointment of losing the juror they had wanted the most. When he'd finished the telling, Mia sensed that Dan was pleased.

While sitting with Mia in their happy place, a sense of contentment washed over Dan, partly from his day being over, partly from the cocktail, but mainly from Mia's presence.

Over the remainder of the evening, she would cook him a wonderful dinner, make love with him tenderly, and fall asleep in his arms. *What did I ever do…?*

**THE COURTHOUSE STEPS** were once again packed with reporters, vying for a sound bite for their viewers. Dan found Joe and Ariana in the lobby and took a seat on a bench. They made small talk to relieve the tension they all felt. Soon, they were joined by their legal team, who had been presenting pretrial briefs to Judge Ferris. After Joe introduced Ariana to everyone, Seth explained how the trial would proceed.

"After opening arguments, the prosecution will present its case first. Then we'll present ours, followed by the prosecution's rebuttal. We know from the witness list that they will be calling one of the original pilots on the aircraft and a few legal experts to explain their interpretation of the law. We will have the opportunity to question their witnesses. Then it will be our turn.

"We'll be calling someone who was held with Ariana, but not you, Ariana, don't worry. Your testimony would be viewed as biased. We'll also present a constitutional law professor from NYU, who will explain the immigrants' rights to due process, which we believe were violated. Our last witness will be a hijacking expert from the NTSB.

"Dan and Joe, we have no intention of calling either of you to testify, so you can also rest easy. Finally, there will be closing arguments before the case goes to the jury. Because of the short witness list, I don't expect the trial to take more than a few days."

Joyce added, "As I've mentioned before, let me know if either of you gets a dirty look from a juror. We may be able to tailor our presentation for them. As the case goes on, you may find the jurors looking at you. If your eyes meet, don't look away quickly; instead, think friendly thoughts and casually move on."

Moments later, the courtroom doors opened, and everyone filed in. Again, everyone stood as instructed by the bailiff when Judge Ferris entered the courtroom. Joe turned to Ariana, seated directly behind him, and they exchanged smiles.

Once Judge Ferris was seated, he asked the bailiff to call the jury in. The judge welcomed everyone and reviewed the rules of his courtroom, warning that he would not tolerate any noise from the gallery. He then welcomed Josh Volpe for his opening statement. Josh listed the charges the defendants were facing and how he intended to prove guilt for each charge. He explained how the people he called to the witness stand would corroborate that guilt. It was a brief and to-the-point opening, without any levity or attempt to establish a connection with the jurors.

When it was Seth's turn, he asked the jurors with a smile if, during the selection, he'd proven he was old enough to perform the duties of an attorney.

He received nods and smiles in response as he made eye contact with most of them. He went on to explain that the defense would prove the laws the prosecution was attempting to enforce violated the Constitution and that, had it not been for the defendant's actions, grave and irreversible injustices would have occurred. He closed by thanking them for their attention.

Judge Ferris announced, "The prosecution may proceed."

Josh called William Wansker to the stand. After being sworn in, Josh introduced him as the pilot of the plane that Joe and Dan were accused of hijacking. The prosecution was using this eyewitness testimony to establish what had occurred on the aircraft. Josh simply asked him to explain the events of that evening. He told the story as he remembered it without embellishment. When Josh asked if he was afraid at the time, the pilot replied, "I was afraid of losing my job if I didn't comply with the orders from someone I believed was an Air Force Colonel."

It was then the defense's turn to question the witness. It had been previously decided that Webb would question this witness. Not just because of his military experience, but because they wanted the jury to become accustomed to him asking questions.

"Mr. Wansker, are you a member of the military?"

"Not anymore."

"How long has it been since you served?"

"I retired five years ago."

"You're now a civilian pilot?"

"A commercial pilot, to be precise. I'm employed by Immigration and Customs Enforcement."

"So you no longer have to obey a senior officer?"

"Well, I have a boss."

"Did the defendants brandish any weapons, or threaten you physically if you did not comply?"

"No, sir."

"What was the intended destination of the flight that morning?"

"Joint Base Andrews, to meet another flight to Qatar."

A few muffled gasps were heard from the gallery, followed by a stern look from the judge.

"That's all I have, Your Honor," Webb said.

"You may redirect, Mr. Volpe."

"Mr. Wansker, why did you turn over the plane to the defendants if you weren't physically threatened?"

"They told me they were ordered by the President to fly to a location that I wasn't qualified to know about."

"And you believed them."

"Yes, because of his uniform, I was convinced he was a senior officer."

"Thank you, I have nothing more," Josh said, returning to his seat.

The Judge said, "You may step down, Mr. Wansker."

Josh Volpe then called Charles Hains to the stand. After being sworn in, Josh asked what his current occupation was.

"I'm a senior fellow at the Federalist Society."

"And what is the Federalist Society?"

"We are a group of legal scholars who, among other things, provide information to the President and Congress about prospective judges they may be considering for appointment."

"I see. Did the Federalist Society recommend the last three Supreme Court nominees?"

"Yes, that's correct."

"Where and when did you obtain your law degree, Mr. Hains?"

"From Princeton University in 1975."

"Could you tell the court about your judicial experience?"

Charles Hains went on to list all his positions, starting with his time as a prosecutor in New York, to his appointment as a circuit court judge, and then on to his appointment to the Superior Court.

When asked when he stepped down from the bench, he replied, "2015. I returned to my alma mater as a professor."

"Do you consider yourself knowledgeable regarding the law?" Josh asked.

Seth stood and said, "Your Honor, to save time, we'll stipulate that Mr. Haines is a qualified expert regarding the legal aspects of the case before us."

"Thank you, Mr. Bodner. You may proceed, Mr. Volpe."

Josh continued, "There have been a lot of opinions of late about Presidential powers. Can you clear that up for us today?"

"I'll try. Article Two of the Constitution defines the powers of the Presidency. It states that the President is required to take care that the laws are faithfully executed, including the authority to enforce and administer laws, among other things. I believe that is the section of Article Two that has come into question."

"Since the defense considers you qualified as an expert in these matters, would you interpret those powers for us today?"

Seth and Webb smiled at each other.

"Well, it's really quite simple. The President and his executive officers shall enforce the laws of this nation. Nothing more, nothing less."

"Thank you, Mr. Hains," Josh said, returning to his seat.

"Defense counsel may approach the witness."

Seth stood, took a few steps around the table, and said, "Mr. Hains, does the Constitution *refute* the idea that the President was intended to be a lawmaker, and in fact grants only Congress the authority to make laws?"

"That is correct."

"Regarding the President's authority, is it not that he *faithfully* executes the laws, and is it not the word *faithfully* that has come into question of late?"

"Perhaps."

"Does the Presidential oath of office require him to preserve, protect, and defend the Constitution?"

"It does."

"Thank you. I have nothing more, Your Honor."

"Mr. Volpe, you may redirect."

Josh stood behind the table and said, "Just to be perfectly clear, Mr. Hains, the Constitution does grant the President and his appointed officials the power to enforce our laws."

"Yes, it does."

"Thank you. That's all I have, Your Honor."

After the witness stepped down, the judge called for a lunch recess and asked everyone to return to their seats by 1:30.

AS HAD BECOME their habit, the defense gathered in a booth at the luncheonette, this time at a round table for six. After asking Ariana what she thought of the trial, she replied simply, "I'm fascinated. Especially how each side asks questions of the same witness, resulting in different answers."

Webb congratulated Seth on forcing the prosecution's witness to make the defense's point about Congressional powers. "Yeah, and we also learned the plane's intended destination. That was a risk they took in putting him on the stand," Seth added.

The conversation turned to what to expect in the afternoon's testimony. After everyone placed their orders, Seth said, "They only have one more witness. I would guess the prosecution will be done today."

"I hope Judge Ferris doesn't expect us to begin this afternoon. Our witnesses aren't scheduled until tomorrow," Webb said.

"He should be aware of that," Seth stated.

"I've been reviewing some of the jury information," Joyce said. "There are still a few that may have lost loved ones on 9/11 that we don't know about."

Dan offered, "I'll try to fill in those blanks this afternoon."


BACK IN THE courtroom, when the jury had been seated, Joe and Ariana acknowledged each other again, hoping the jury would notice. Then the prosecution called their last witness, Harold Chambers, an immigration law professor from John Jay College of Criminal Justice.

After going through his credentials, much like he did with the Federalist Society member, and without objection from the defense, Josh Volpe asked, "Why are illegal immigrants being detained in such large numbers over the last few months?"

"Because the new President and his administration have ordered their deportation."

"Has this been a change in policy from the last administration?"

"Absolutely. Under the previous administration, ICE only deported criminals and gang members, along with those who were arrested and discovered to be undocumented."

"Do you know why the new administration changed the policy?"

"I believe it's just the sheer number of undocumented immigrants that are here."

"Seth stood and said, "Objection, Your Honor."

"Go ahead, Mr. Bodner."

"This witness has no direct knowledge of why policies are made."

Josh spun toward the judge and said, "Your Honor, it's public knowledge that there are too many undocumented immigrants here."

"The objection is sustained," Judge Ferris stated. "Neither you nor the professor has the authority to decide how many is too many, and it would be hearsay for the witness to know the intent of the administration. Move on, Mr. Volpe."

After swallowing the admonishment, Josh asked the witness, "How many undocumented immigrants have been detained or deported since the change of administrations?"

"By last count, it was in excess of two hundred fifty thousand."

"Thank you, Professor. That's all I have at this time, Your Honor."

"Mr. Bodner?"

Seth rose, approached the stand, and asked, "Do you know how many of the detainees have been granted a hearing before being deported?"

"I don't know a number, but some were and some were not."

"Why would some not receive a hearing?"

"I've heard the President say himself that there isn't time to have a hearing for everyone."

"Since you are an immigration professor, is it not the law that every immigrant receives due process before being deported?"

"Technically, yes. But the President has declared an emergency, and claims he has a mandate from the voters to act."

"Since you seem to know what the President is thinking, if these people ended up in Qatar, would he have notified the families of their location?"

"That, I couldn't say."

"That's all I have, Your Honor."

"Anything else, Mr. Volpe?"

"No, Your Honor."

"You may step down, professor."

"Mr. Volpe, I see that you have no more witnesses on your list?"

"That's correct, Your Honor."

"Thank you, everyone. This court is in recess until 10:00 tomorrow."

**IT WAS NOT** quite 3:00 when everyone exited the courtroom. Before leaving, Joyce handed Dan the list of jurors for whom she wanted additional information.

She, Seth, and Webb exited through the side, while Dan, Joe, and Ariana faced the mob outside on the steps. Joe managed to protect his wife from being struck in the face with a microphone, but all the viewers of the evening news would see her walk out with Joe. Before leaving the lot, Dan texted Mia that he was on his way.

There, like the day before, Mia was waiting to hear about Dan's day in court. While sipping Manhattans, Dan replayed the scene in the courtroom, noting that the prosecution had finished presenting its case and that tomorrow would be the defense's turn.

"I have some homework to do. Should I do it before or after dinner?" he asked.

"Before. Then I can have you all to myself for the rest of the evening."

"I like that idea," Dan replied. "But first, let's finish our drinks."

The afternoon sun was still strong, and the New York skyline appeared dark as the sun crept lower behind it. A while later, when their glasses were empty, Mia asked, "How much time do you need?"

"An hour and a half should be plenty."

"All right, I'll time dinner accordingly."


**DAN SAT DOWN** at the dining room table with Joyce's list, his laptop, and the notebook he'd created for the case. He thumbed through to make sure the 9/11 information wasn't already there—maybe he'd missed transcribing it to the jury list. He had not.

After conducting a Google search of the jurors' surnames, nothing came up about 9/11 for any of the three. Since one of them was female, he glanced at the list, saw that she was married, and knew he'd need her maiden name to complete the search. That information was not in the jurors' questionnaire.

Knowing her age and the ages of her children, he first searched through marriage announcements and then birth announcements, which were often listed in local papers for the state of New York, for a maiden name. Finding nothing, Dan tried the neighboring states, New Jersey and Connecticut. Still nothing.

Lastly, Dan went back to social media using her married name, knowing that some women list their maiden names there as well, as if it were a middle name. While he found her on Facebook and Instagram, there was no mention of a maiden name. However, her Facebook bio listed the high school she attended, and through an online database, Dan was able to view high school yearbooks for the years he estimated she would have graduated. There, he scrolled through looking for her by first name, Elizabeth, hoping to recognize her from the picture.

After scanning through three years of yearbooks, there were a couple of dozen Elizabeths that he couldn't rule out. But the yearbooks were from twenty to twenty-three years ago, and people's faces change too much between seventeen and forty years old. Having already spent nearly an hour on this one person, Dan moved on to the men.

There, he found the process relatively simple. Dan scanned the database of people who were killed on 9/11, looking for anyone with the same last name. I found none for either of them, no parents, uncles, or brothers. While it was still possible to have lost a sister who took her husband's name, he felt that he'd exhausted every possibility.

Having a few minutes left before dinner, Dan's mind went back to the woman. Since he'd already located the yearbooks, he scrolled through them looking for her married name, thinking it possible that she'd married someone she went to high school with. Nothing. A moment later, Mia called him to dinner.

# CHAPTER 25

As the morning sun peeked through the curtains, Dan found himself still troubled by his inability to find Elizabeth's maiden name. He was just too tenacious by nature to give up and accept defeat, yet after another round on the computer, he had still come up empty.

While eating breakfast with Mia, they watched the local news. There was a new story out of Washington that had replaced the trial as the lead story. It seemed that the President was more closely involved with a pedophile than previously thought. The reporters promised more as the day unfolded, before moving on to their trial. Dan was pleased that another news story had finally bumped them from the lead. They watched clips of yesterday's scene on the courthouse steps, along with sketch artists' renderings of him and Joe. One sketch of Joe showed Ariana sitting behind him in the courtroom. The artist had taken the liberty of sketching Ariana as being in anguish. There were also legal experts discussing the case, each trying to speculate what the turning point in the trial would be.

After a kiss and a hug from Mia, Dan headed for the courthouse. There, during their huddle in the lobby, Dan told Joyce that the two male jurors had no family members involved on 9/11. He then asked if she knew of any way to find the maiden name of the female juror.

"Yes, I can ask the judge to have the jurors provide any alias they have used in the past, and maiden names would qualify."

Dan was instantly relieved. While they wouldn't have the 9/11 information that day, he was confident he'd have it for the next.

After Joyce passed a note to the bailiff, the trial continued in the fashion they had become accustomed to, except this time, it would be Seth and Webb presenting their case. As Seth rose to call the first witness, he had a quick quip for the jury, raising a smile from each of them. It was obvious that the jurors liked him.

His first witness was Thomas Mann, a professor of constitutional law at George Washington University.

After summarizing his qualifications, Seth opened the questioning with, "Professor Mann, is there a law in the United States that guarantees a person's right to due process?"

"Yes. The Fifth Amendment to the Constitution says no one shall be 'deprived of life, liberty, or property without due process of law' by the federal government."

"Thank you, I recall that from law school." Again, he got a smile from the jurors. "Does that amendment distinguish between citizens of the United States

and a non-citizen?"

"No, it does not. It reads, 'No one shall be.'"

"In the many years since the Constitution was written, has the Supreme Court ever heard cases that challenged that law?"

"Certainly. The Supreme Court has extensively ruled on who qualifies for Fifth Amendment protections. The Due Process Clause applies to all individuals within U.S. territory, including aliens, and protects them from being deprived of life, liberty, or property without due process of law. I may have repeated myself, but the rulings are unambiguous."

"Thank you, Professor. Are you familiar with the case before us today?"

"I am."

"In your professional opinion, what would have happened to the people aboard the plane had they not been rescued by the defendants?"

Josh Volpe stood. "Objection, Your Honor, the witness cannot possibly predict the future."

"Overruled. The witness has been asked to provide an opinion, not a fact. You may answer the question, Professor," Judge Ferris stated.

"Besides being denied their rights, they may never have been heard from again," the Professor answered.

"Thank you, Professor. That's all I have," Seth concluded.

"Mr. Volpe, you may approach the witness stand," the judge said.

"Professor, are you aware of the emergency powers granted to the President by law?"

"Yes. The National Emergency Act was passed in 1976 to address concerns about the potential for *abuse* of emergency powers."

"Is a Declared National Emergency in effect at the present time?"

"Yes. The new President declared a national emergency regarding our southern border on January 20th of this year."

"Thank you, Professor," Josh said before returning to the prosecution table.

"Mr. Bodner, you may redirect."

"Thank you, Your Honor."

"Professor, what authority does the current National Emergency Declaration grant the President?" Seth asked.

"It primarily grants him the power to call the military into action to protect the border."

"Does it grant him the power to suspend rights guaranteed under the Fifth Amendment?

"Absolutely not."

"Thank you," Seth said while returning to his seat.

"The witness may step down," the judge said.

Once Professor Mann had left the courtroom, Seth announced. "The defense calls Farah Noor to the witness stand."

The bailiff opened the doors to the lobby and escorted the witness in.

In most cases, witnesses were not allowed to hear prior testimony. Once she was seated and sworn in, Seth asked his first question. "Ms. Noor, can you tell the court about your experience with ICE beginning on April 27th of this year?"

Appearing nervous, she took a deep breath to calm herself, and Seth told her to take her time and, if she became upset, she could take a break.

"Okay," Ms. Noor began. "I was with my daughter at Pascone Park for the annual Eid celebration. For those who are unfamiliar, Eid is a religious holiday observed by the Muslim faith that can last anywhere from a few days to a few weeks each year. Anyway, as we were leaving, we were stopped by ICE agents and told to get into a van. My daughter had no idea what was happening."

Farah Noor's testimony took nearly an hour, as she recounted the story of how they had been taken to the local police station, then transferred overnight to the prison in Orange County. She spoke about how attorney Bodner visited them there and arranged for a hearing with an immigration judge the following day. She recalled how relieved they were to have a hearing scheduled and assumed they'd be released since all of them were documented and the children were citizens.

While Farah fought back tears, Ariana began crying in the gallery, which was noticed by the jury. Farah then recounted how they had been woken in the middle of the night, loaded onto a bus, then an airplane, and transported to an unknown place in central Florida, where they were again bused to a prison. She told of the stifling heat and humidity inside the prison.

Farah recalled how she had lost track of the days and of her deep concern for her daughter, who was born in the United States. She went on to speak of a new hearing that had been held in the prison, which Seth had arranged, and the joy that overcame them when the judge ordered their release. But within a minute, the prosecutor challenged the judge with an appeal that would require them to spend one more night in that horrid place. While disappointed, they clung to the hope they'd be released the following day.

She then recounted being woken up again in the middle of the night and being loaded onto a bus. She recalled being cuffed and shackled, and began sobbing uncontrollably, before exclaiming, "And so was my five-year-old daughter!"

When it appeared she would not recover quickly, Judge Ferris called for the lunch recess. Ariana was in tears as well, and Joe turned in his seat to comfort her. All this was seen by the jury as they filed out.

Seth escorted Farah to the lobby, where Ariana rushed to hug her, and they both sobbed. When they had settled down, Ariana invited Farah to join them for lunch. When Farah hesitated, Seth insisted that she join them, and Ariana led her by the hand to the luncheonette across the street.

At the big round table, Seth told Farah how well she'd done, how he felt the trial had turned in their favor due to her testimony, and that she only had a little more to go. After ordering, Ariana and Farah chatted while the attorneys planned the afternoon. The mood among the attorneys was upbeat, with Joyce commenting on how riveted the jury was by Farah's story.

**AFTER RETURNING TO** the courtroom, the bailiff brought a copy of the completed alias questionnaire to both tables. After a quick review, Joyce passed it to Dan. When the judge was seated and saw that Farah had regained her composure, he asked the bailiff to recall the jury. When they were seated, he reminded Farah that she was still under oath, and Seth recounted where she'd left off, asking her to continue.

"While on the plane, we were all horrified by where we would be taken next. We'd heard about the prison in El Salvador and thought the worst.

About half an hour after takeoff, a pilot in uniform came out of the cockpit, walked down the aisle, and sat next to Ariana. When she threw her arms around him, I wondered what was going on, but then Ariana announced to all of us that the pilot was her husband and he would rescue us. I'd never felt relief like I did at that moment. Before he returned to the cockpit, he informed us that we'd be back in New York in a few hours, and our families had been notified of where to pick us up. When my daughter and I hugged, I've never felt such joy in my life."

"Thank you, Ms. Noor. That's all I have," Seth stated.

"Mr. Volpe, do you have questions for this witness?"

"No, Your Honor."

"Next witness, Mr. Bodner."

"Your Honor, if it pleases the court, I'd like Mr. Webber to interview this witness."

"Certainly."

"The defense calls Matthew Griffith to the stand," Webb announced.

The bailiff escorted the witness into the courtroom and then administered the oath.

"Mr. Griffith, would you state your occupation, please?" Webb asked in his fatherly manner.

"I am newly retired from the National Transportation Safety Board."

"That's the organization that investigates accidents, correct?"

"Yes, commonly known as the NTSB. We also investigate other occurrences related to airplanes and other modes of transportation."

"Did you have an area of specialty while at the NTSB?"

"Yes. I was the lead investigator of hijackings since 1980. I also investigated the D.B. Cooper hijacking during my first year on the job."

"Is that the one where he jumped from the rear exit of a 727 and was never found?"

"It is."

"Is there a common element to all hijackings?"

"Well, in every case, the hijacker threatened someone with physical harm if they did not alter the flight of the aircraft."

"Were they all armed?"

"If you mean with a gun, some were and some were not. If you recall the hijacking on 9/11, they used box cutters."

"Have you ever investigated a hijacking where no weapon was used and there was no threat to someone's safety?"

"No. Even if there was no weapon visible, there was a bomb threat."

"So, if someone were to take an airplane without any threat to personal safety or the safety of the aircraft, would you consider that a hijacking?"

"No. I would consider it theft if they did not have permission from the owner of the aircraft."

"Thank you. That's all I have, Your Honor."

"Mr. Volpe?"

Josh Volpe stood and approached the witness. "Mr. Griffith, are you familiar with the events of this case?"

"Thoroughly."

"Are you aware that the defendants have been charged with hijacking by the Justice Department of the United States?"

"I am."

"What makes you think that you know more about the law than they do?"

"I merely expressed my opinion as an experienced hijacking expert. As for the Justice Department, they often interpret the law politically."

Clearly perturbed, Josh Volpe challenged, "So you think these charges were made up for political purposes?"

"I didn't say that. There may have been a crime committed; I just don't think it was a hijacking."

"I'm done with this witness, Your Honor," Josh announced as he returned to his seat in a huff.

"Mr. Webber?"

"I have nothing more, Your Honor."

"Mr. Bodner, I see you've called all your listed witnesses. Do you have anything else for the court?"

"No, Your Honor. The defense rests."

"Mr. Volpe. Do you have any rebuttal witnesses?"

"No, sir. The prosecution rests."

"All right then. I'll give counsel the rest of the day to prepare for closing arguments. The court is in recess until tomorrow at 10:00."

As most of the courtroom filed out, the defense table remained to discuss plans for the next day. During the first two days of the trial, Joyce had been observing the jurors and had seen no visible clues of hatred from any of them. Seth and Webb felt very good about how the day had gone. Their first witness had presented a much more compelling interpretation of the law than the prosecution's legal scholar. Farah had told the story of their detainment beyond their wildest imagination, having captured the juror's attention, and as far as they could tell, their sympathy as well. Their final witness had exasperated Josh Volpe enough that the jury noticed it.

Before leaving, it was decided that Seth would handle the closing arguments because of the rapport he had established with the jury. With everyone in a positive state of mind, they all filed out and went their own ways.

# CHAPTER 26

I arrived at Mia's a bit earlier than expected, while she was in the middle of a project. With some more research to do on the one remaining Juror's 9/11 connection, I sat down with my laptop and went to work. Knowing now that the juror's maiden name was Vona, I conducted a Google search and then a social media search for any information related to 9/11. There was nothing.

Lastly, I accessed the 9/11 victim database and scrolled through the alphabet until I reached the V's. Va, Ve, Vi, Vo, Vol, Vom, Von, there was no Vona to be found. But staring me in the face was Volpe. Two of them, while it wasn't an unusual name, it wasn't particularly common either, so I dug a little deeper. Ralph and Janet Volpe, both of the same address in Queens.

I then Googled them with immediate confirmation that they were both employed in the World Trade Center and had both died when the buildings collapsed. There were multiple references to newspaper articles, and when I clicked on the links, I found stories about their community associations and finally their obituary. It was there that I found they were survived by both a daughter and a son, Lori and Josh.

My heart palpitated, and a feeling washed over me, a feeling I'd felt before when I'd finally found the missing piece of the puzzle that solved a crime. Squashing my excitement, I found the age of the children, and with young Josh at twelve years old in 2001, he'd now be thirty-six, give or take a year, certainly in line with the prosecutor I'd been sharing a courtroom with for the last week.

Now my excitement was irrepressible. I began the search all over again, this time targeting Josh Volpe. His bio on Facebook showed him growing up in Queens, graduating from law school, and passing the bar exam in 2014. After a few years with the State prosecutors' office, he became a federal prosecutor for the Southern District of New York. I was convinced it was the same Josh Volpe, and a publicity photo confirmed it.

*"Holy shit,"* I said out loud.

From her office across the foyer, Mia said, "What's that, love?"

With my excitement piqued, I ran to her door and exclaimed, "I just found out the prosecutor is biased! He lost his parents on 9/11, and there's no way he should have been assigned to a case involving Muslims."

Mia understood the bias immediately and asked, "What are you going to do?"

"I have to inform Seth," I replied, as excited as Mia had ever seen me.

"All right, I'll make the cocktails while you do that."

"Okay, sweetheart. Thanks."

Taking a few calming breaths, I made the call. Fortunately, Seth answered after a few rings.

As I'd been trained by the NYPD many years ago, I reported the facts as I knew them, in chronological order, while Seth, who'd remained silent, took it all in. It was only when I'd finished that he asked questions. After a few moments, Seth said, "Shit. This throws our entire case out the window."

Shocked by his response, I said, "What do you mean? I thought this would be good news."

"It is Dan, and good work. But we'll have to inform the judge, and he'll rule for a mistrial. We couldn't have presented a better case than we did this week. I've never felt better about a case—we had the jury eating out of our hands. Now we'll have to try it all over again, with a new jury, and the prosecution will know our strong points and their weak ones. We had this in the bag, Dan."

*Shit! Why didn't I see this coming? I could have kept it to myself,* I thought before saying, "Okay, could we just not tell the judge?"

"Not if I ever want to work as an attorney again. Sandbagging a judge is a big no-no."

"All right, man. I'm sure you know best."

"No worries. Email me a copy of the evidence, and I'll discuss it with Webb. We'll see what we come up with."

Mia had overheard my side of the conversation and watched my elation turn to gloom. After the call ended, I filled her in, and she understood the predicament entirely.

While sipping our drinks in the kitchen as Mia prepared dinner, I turned on the TV, hoping to catch a news story about the case. Instead, it was all about the President. The breaking news we heard that morning, about the President and the pedophile, had gone viral.

Later that evening, I received a text from Seth requesting that I come to his office at 8:00 a.m. for another strategy session.

# CHAPTER 27

Paula welcomed Dan with a cup of coffee when he walked in, then opened the door to the conference room, where Seth and Webb were already deep in conversation. A moment later, Joe arrived.

"Thanks for coming in early," Seth said. "Let me bring Joe up to speed."

Seth told Joe about what Dan had discovered regarding the lead prosecutor and how it affected the case. As he explained what would happen if a mistrial were declared, Joe understood the gravity of the situation and the loss of what the attorneys felt was a near-certain acquittal.

Webb chimed in, "We're about to have our victory snatched away from us, and then have to face a retrial that may not go as well for us. Seth and I have a proposal: Would you be willing to plead guilty to a misdemeanor charge, with no jail time?"

Joe and Dan's shoulders slumped, and a sour look came over their faces. They were both speechless for a moment before Dan said, "Are you certain we need to tell the judge? What if we say I never told you?"

"I'm certain," Seth said. "And no, we can't just say that."

"I agree," Webb added.

"What about my PI license?" Dan asked.

"A misdemeanor won't have an effect on your license," Seth replied.

Webb added, "If this offer had been made to us two days ago, we would have jumped at it."

Seth nodded in agreement, gauging his client's reaction. "We'll give you guys a few minutes to discuss it." He and Webb left the room.

"What do you think, Joe?"

"I don't know. I was expecting to walk out of court today with a verdict of 'not guilty.'"

"What if the judge or the prosecution won't go along with it?"

"I don't know, shall we ask our attorneys?"

They both thought for a few moments. "Yeah. Let's get 'em back in here," Joe concluded.

Dan opened the door and gestured for them to return.

"What if they won't accept our plea?" Dan asked.

"Then nothing lost, nothing gained. It will be in the hands of the judge."

"I'm in," Joe said.

"Whatever you recommend, Seth," I concurred.

"Good, we'll give it a try," Seth said. "I already told Judge Ferris to expect us early."


WHEN THEY ARRIVED at the courthouse, there wasn't yet a crowd on the steps. Seth led Dan and Joe to an attorney's conference room while he and Webb continued down the hall to meet with Judge Ferris.

Seth knocked on the judge's door and heard, "Come in."

"Thank you for seeing us, judge. We came across something last night that needs to be brought to your attention," Seth said, handing the judge the emailed copies.

They watched as the judge's eyes widened in surprise. "You know what this means, don't you?"

"We believe we do."

"I'm forced to call for a mistrial, that son of a bitch. Did he think he was going to get away with this? I'll refer him to the Bar!"

"We agree, Judge. But we have a proposal that may alleviate a mistrial."

"I'm all ears, Counselors."

"What if our clients plead guilty to a lesser charge?"

"And what would that charge be?"

"A misdemeanor charge of 'unauthorized use of an airplane.'"

"With a suspended sentence, I presume?"

"Of course."

"You were clearly winning the case, counselors. Why are you offering a plea?"

"No one wants to go through the process of a retrial, Your Honor. Not us, not our clients, and if I were to venture a guess, not the court either."

"True," Judge Ferris said, shaking his head, clearly troubled. After a minute of deep thought, a smile came over his face. "I have another idea. This is highly improper, but take your evidence with you and submit it to the bailiff along with a written argument during jury deliberations. We'll bring Volpe in now, and you present your plea deal. If he doesn't accept it, we continue with the trial. In the off chance that there's a guilty verdict, I'll use your evidence to declare a mistrial."

Dan and Webb looked at each other, realizing the judge had gone way out on a limb and handed them a win-win situation.

"You did the right thing here, Counselors; you deserve to be rewarded. If this goes the way I think it will, Volpe will not only lose this trial, but will lose his career as well."

Judge Ferris picked up his phone, rang the bailiff, and said, "When you see Mr. Volpe, send him in, please. Have a seat, gentlemen. He should be here shortly."

A minute later, Josh Volpe stuck his head in the door and said, "You wanted to see me, Your Honor?"

"Yes, please come in."

When Josh saw Seth and Webb already in the judge's chambers, he knew something was up.

"The defense has a plea deal they'd like to offer," said the judge.

Josh looked over at Seth and Webb and said, "Let's hear it." When Seth explained it to him, Josh smiled, "A misdemeanor? For those charges? You've got to be joking."

Judge Ferris said, "Listen, Mr. Volpe, if the jury decides the case, I'm betting that you'll lose."

"I wouldn't be so sure about that," Volpe said.

"Do you want to discuss this offer with the district attorney?"

"No, thanks. I know what he'll say."

"Very well. I'll see you in the courtroom at 10:00, Counsellors."

On the way to the lobby, Seth and Webb stopped to retrieve Dan and Joe from the conference room. After telling their clients that the prosecutor had rejected their plea deal, Seth said, "Sometimes you're rewarded for doing the right thing."

Dan and Joe cocked their heads and looked at the attorneys.

"Judge Ferris told us to hang onto the evidence and give it to the bailiff during deliberations, along with a written argument," Seth explained.

"No mistrial?" Dan asked.

"Only if we lose."


ARIANA ARRIVED A few minutes before 10:00 and walked into the courtroom, taking a seat in the first row behind her husband. Everyone at the defense table was trying to suppress their elation over the trial's predetermined outcome. Dan glanced around at the full gallery behind them and nodded to Imam Khan sitting on the aisle with a few of the Muslims who'd been detained. There was a sense of excitement in the courtroom, more so than on the previous days.

Once the formalities were out of the way and the judge and jury were seated, Josh Volpe approached the jury. For the first time, he showed some levity, which the jury interpreted as a last-minute attempt to make himself likable. Then he began his closing arguments: "Today you will be asked to decide if the defendants are guilty of four charges, the first being interfering with a government proceeding. Clearly, after hearing the evidence presented in this case, you must agree that they interfered with the Department of Homeland Security and their duty to protect our borders as ordered by the President.

"The second charge is Conspiracy." After taking a book off the prosecution table, Josh Volpe said, "Allow me to read the legal definition of conspiracy: 'A conspiracy is a secret plan or agreement between people, referred to as conspirators, for an unlawful or harmful purpose, such as murder, treason, or corruption, especially with a political motivation, while keeping their agreement secret from the public or from other authorities.' From what you have heard in this courtroom, was there any mention of them sharing their intention of taking control of the airplane with the public or any authority? If not, you *must* find them guilty of conspiracy.

"The third charge is theft of government property. Just ask yourself, did these two men take the airplane without permission? Permission from anyone? Was the plane not government property? That is the definition of theft, plain and simple.

"The fourth charge is hijacking. Have any of you not seen stories of hijacking on the news over the course of your lives? Does this case sound any different? You heard for yourself, from the defendant's own witness, that hijacking is when someone alters the flight of an aircraft from its intended destination. Clearly, they are guilty on that charge."

Walking closer to the jury box, Josh Volpe continued, "Ladies and gentlemen of the jury, you are called upon here today to decide the guilt or innocence of the defendants beyond a reasonable doubt." Holding up the book again, he said, "Allow me to read you the definition of reasonable doubt." After leafing through a few pages, he began, "Reasonable doubt is a rational and logical uncertainty about a defendant's guilt that arises from the evidence presented, or a lack of evidence, preventing a jury from being firmly convinced of guilt. It's not a vague or imaginary doubt, but rather a doubt so significant that a reasonable person would hesitate to act on it in matters of great personal importance."

"I'd like to thank each and every one of you for serving on this jury. It is up to good people like you to uphold the laws of our country. Again, I thank you."

After a few moments, Judge Ferris announced. "The defense may approach the jury."

Seth sprang to his feet, his energy matching the courtroom's, as the jury looked forward to what he'd have to say. Seth began with a brief version of the story of David and Goliath, the symbolism not lost on the jury.

"I'm sure you're all looking forward to this trial being over, and I promise, we are near the end. I'd like you to think back in time, not very long ago, perhaps just a few months, and ask yourselves if any of these events would have occurred—*could* have occurred. Would seven people of the Muslim faith have been snatched off the streets as they were leaving a religious celebration? Legal residents with families present?

"We are here today because of a heinous use of political power, a power so overwhelming that other branches of government are afraid to put a stop to it. Here is an undeniable fact: If they had not been intentionally denied due process as required by the Constitution, none of this would have happened." Seth paused, poured himself a glass of water from a pitcher on the defense table, and took a sip, allowing time for his statement to sink into the minds of the jurors.

"Let me tell you a little bit about Colonel Wilkinson's wife, Ariana, who is sitting in the courtroom today behind her husband."

Unprepared to be put on the spot, Ariana smiled and brushed a few strands of hair from her face, as all eyes focused on her.

"While serving in our military," Seth continued, "Colonel Wilkinson met Ariana in Afghanistan when she was among his staff, who helped with translations and local knowledge. Ariana was one of many Afghan citizens who our soldiers relied upon to keep them safe, while risking their own lives as well as the lives of their families.

"While serving in Afghanistan, Colonel Wilkinson fell in love with Ariana, and they were married. As our military involvement in that war was ending, they arranged for her to fly to the States with the other military families. They followed all the rules, obtained a visa for her entry, and since then, Ariana has become a United States citizen. Additionally, Mr. and Mrs. Wilkinson have welcomed two children into the world, also US citizens. If Ariana were to go back to Afghanistan now, the Taliban would certainly torture and kill her. I ask any one of you, if you were her husband, would you not have done what Colonel Wilkinson did, knowing what was in store for his wife?"

With some in the courtroom dabbing tears from their eyes, Seth continued, "So, getting back to how all this came about, have we seen any European people deported? How about Canadian people? The answer is no. I suggest the entire deportation program put in place by our current President is an act of racism. They like to say they are deporting criminals and gang members. You can look at Ariana Wilkinson or recall Farah Noor, who testified before you yesterday. Do either of them appear to be criminals or gang members? I can tell you with certainty that neither of them has a criminal record, nor do any of the others rounded up outside their religious celebration.

"It may be uncomfortable to admit, but this country has a long history of racial cruelty and prejudice. Today, you have the chance to have your voices heard, once and for all." After making eye contact with every juror, Seth said, "Thank you for your attention."

The gallery began clapping as Seth returned to the table, while Judge Ferris banged his gavel, shouting, "Order in the court!"

Once the courtroom quieted down, Judge Ferris gave the jury their instructions before they filed out to the jury room. Like all cases, no matter how well the defense had presented their case, there was anxiety over the jury's verdict. But on that day, the defense was less concerned.

Before leaving the courtroom, Seth handed the bailiff an envelope addressed to the judge, then joined the others in the lobby, preparing for what awaited them on the courthouse steps. For the first time that week, Seth paused to answer questions, stating that he trusted the jury to return a verdict of not guilty. In response to another question, he repeated a few phrases from his closing argument, his clients smiling with confidence alongside him, while Joe held his wife's hand.

**OVER LUNCH, AFTER** everyone congratulated Seth on his moving speech, Webb predicted a quick verdict. Seth remained silent, waiting for the bailiff's call. Through routine conversation, Dan discovered that Joe was a fellow sailor.

After lunch, while the others were having coffee, Joyce excused herself, saying, "My work is done here."

While everyone thanked her, she wished them good luck as she exited the restaurant at the exact moment that Seth got the call.

"The verdict is in," he announced before picking up the tab.

AS THEY ALL climbed the courthouse steps, the reporters again shouted questions, this time asking, *"What does a quick verdict mean?"* and *"Are you confident?"*

Elsa Nordstrom caught Dan's eye by holding up crossed fingers.

After the gallery filled in, the bailiff closed the door and announced, "All rise," followed by the judge taking his seat.

"Bailiff, call in the jury, please."

As the jury entered, everyone in the room tried to read their eyes for a clue about the verdict. Once they were seated, the judge asked, "Has the jury reached a verdict?"

"We have, Your Honor," the foreperson replied, handing the written verdict to the bailiff.

When it was delivered to Judge Ferris, he glanced at the paper and asked, "As to the charges of interfering with a legal proceeding, how does the jury find?"

"Not guilty, Your Honor."

There were murmurs in the courtroom, prompting the judge to request silence.

"As to the charges of Conspiracy, how does the jury find?"

"Not guilty."

"For the charges of Theft of Government Property, how does the jury find?"

"Not guilty."

More murmurs, another stern look.

"And to the charges of hijacking?"

"Not guilty, Your Honor."

They'd barely gotten the words out before the courtroom erupted, the judge banging his gavel.

When quiet was restored, the judge asked, "Mr. Volpe, would you like me to poll the jurors individually?"

"No, Your Honor," he replied, dejected.

"Members of the jury, the court thanks you for your service. You're dismissed. This court is adjourned," Judge Ferris announced with a final bang of the gavel.

Everyone at the defense table hugged and congratulated each other. Joe leaned over the rail, hugging Ariana, while Dan texted Mia with the verdict: *Not guilty on all counts.*

This time, as they descended the courthouse steps, Joe, Dan, and their attorneys stopped to speak with the media, answering their questions and posing for photographs. Elsa Nordstrom sought out Dan, and he took his time answering all her questions. He introduced Elsa to Joe and Ariana, and Elsa asked her what it was like after being held captive to see the verdict go their way.

Ariana replied, "Joe always told me how great America was. I'll admit to having some doubts there for a while, but he was right."

# EPILOGUE

When I got home, Mia was waiting with a bottle of champagne on ice in our happy place. After a long embrace, I popped the cork and poured two flutes. I told her about the plea deal we'd offered, the prosecution's refusal, and how Seth had managed to work things out with the judge over the evidence of bias.

When I'd left that morning, we were expecting a mistrial. But Mia had followed the whole day on TV and knew how it went down.

After a second glass, we carried the bottle upstairs and spent the rest of the afternoon in her oversized bathtub, melting away the tension of the last few weeks. We never left the bedroom that evening, except when Mia brought up a tray of strawberries she had earlier dipped in chocolate, with another bottle of champagne. Between rounds of lovemaking, we talked about summer plans—sailing *Privateer* to Nantucket, anchoring off Martha's Vineyard, and forgetting, for a while, how close we'd come to losing faith in the system.

**A FEW WEEKS** later, a short item appeared deep in the pages of *The New York Times*: the prosecutor in the so-called Muslim hijacking trial had been disbarred for improper conduct. It never made the network news. Too small a story in a country drowning in bigger issues. But I read it twice, folded the paper, and smiled. Justice doesn't always roar in the headlines. Sometimes it whispers, just loud enough for those who need to hear it.

Thank you for reading *Tracking Ariana*


If you enjoyed the book, please leave an Amazon Review!


You may follow the author at
www.larryterhaar.com


*Other titles by this Author:*


**Against the Blue Wall** https://a.co/d/2duKj5p
**Once a Detective...** https://a.co/d/jf0pO3n
**Oceanside** https://a.co/d/eAMb3cG
**Breath Play** https://a.co/d/4wTS8TW

# ACKNOWLEGEMENTS

My sincere thanks to all those who helped me bring this book
to publication.

Proofreading by Larry Butler

Formatting by Trisha Fuentes

Book Cover by Zizi Subiyarta

My advanced reading team for posting early reviews

(You know who you are.)

A special thanks to my editor, Emma Collins

As always, I dedicate this book to my wife, Beth, whose support makes everything possible.